JUSTICE

A lost relic.

A pirate's treasure.

A mystery from the time of America's Founding Fathers.

A break-in at Mount Vernon sets Dane Maddock and Bones Bonebrake on an action-packed search for the lost treasure of the most notorious pirates in history, and once again hurls them into the path of the Sons of the Republic. From famous landmarks to secret passages, danger lurks around every corner as Maddock and Bones race to find JUSTICE!

Praise for David Wood and the Dane Maddock Adventures

"Dane and Bones.... Together they're unstoppable. Rip roaring action from start to finish. Wit and humor throughout. Just one question - how soon until the next one? Because I can't wait." **Graham Brown, author of** *Shadows of the Midnight Sun*

"What an adventure! A great read that provides lots of action, and thoughtful insight as well, into strange realms that are sometimes best left unexplored." **Paul Kemprecos, author of** *Cool Blue Tomb* **and the** *NUMA Files*

"A brisk read, reminiscent of early Cussler adventures, and perfect for an afternoon at the beach or a cross-country flight. You'll definitely want more of Maddock**." Sean Ellis-Author of** *Into the Black*

"A non-stop thrill ride triple threat- smart, funny and mysterious." **Jeremy Robinson, author of** *Threshold*

"David Wood has done it again. Quest takes you on an expedition that leads down a trail of adventure and thrills. David Wood has honed his craft and Quest is proof of his efforts!" **David L. Golemon, Author of the *Event Group* series.**

"Ancient cave paintings? Cities of gold? Secret scrolls? Sign me up! Cibola is a twisty tale of adventure and intrigue that never lets up and never lets go!" -**Robert Masello, author of *The Einstein Prophecy*.**

JUSTICE

A Dane and Bones Origins Story

DAVID WOOD
EDWARD G. TALBOT

Gryphonwood

JUSTICE

Published by Gryphonwood Press
Copyright 2016 by David Wood
All rights reserved.
Cover by Stan Tremblay

ISBN-10: 1-940095-45-X
ISBN-13: 978-1-940095-45-5

Works by David Wood

The Dane Maddock Adventures
Dourado
Cibola
Quest
Icefall
Buccaneer
Atlantis
Ark

Dane and Bones Origins
Freedom
Hell Ship
Splashdown
Dead Ice
Liberty
Electra
Amber
Justice

Jade Ihara Adventures
Oracle
Changeling

Myrmidon Files
Destiny

Brock Stone Adventures
Arena of Souls

Bones Bonebrake Adventures
Primitive
The Book of Bones (forthcoming)

Works by Edward G. Talbot

Alive From New York (Terrorist Chronicles Book One)
Alive From America (Terrorist Chronicles Book Two)

2012: The Fifth World
New World Orders

Rook (with Jeremy Robinson)
Liberty (with David Wood)
Justice (with David Wood

From the Authors

Mark Twain said, "Never let the truth stand in the way of a good story" and who are we to argue. As usual, we've included many details, both contemporary and historical, that we hope will add to your enjoyment of the story, but we've also changed or created a few things for the sake of the story. Thanks for coming along on another adventure with Maddock and Bones. We hope you enjoy it!

David and Edward

PROLOGUE

May 30, 1431
Rouen, France

Jehanne la Pucelle felt the heat of the flames licking her feet. She stood bound to a pole on a wooden platform resting atop four feet of stacked logs. Beneath and around the logs lay a small amount of straw, just enough to kindle the slower burning wood. The Incuisitors claimed that this precaution contained the blaze inside the circling crowd. The real reason was to avoid having the fumes from a larger blaze render the victim unconscious well before death. Heretics deserved prolonged punishment. It was justice.

Jehanne knew she would suffer, but it would be short compared to the eternal reward that awaited her. She only wished it would end soon. As if in response to this thought, a voice spoke to her.

"Child, it does not please God for you to welcome death."

Jehanne's eyes opened at the welcome sound. St. Catherine had spoken to her nearly every day since Jehanne reached the age of twelve, a constant presence who had driven her to lead the armies of the French King Charles VII. St. Margaret appeared nearly as often. Many did not believe that Jehanne truly heard the words of the saints, but the voices had correctly predicted the outcome of numerous battles, including the conflict resulting in her own capture a year earlier.

"Forgive me."

She heard no reply. Her mind drifted, focusing on the one thing which had increasingly dominated her thoughts in the previous months. Jehanne was protecting a secret; one revealed by St. Michael himself shortly after she began hearing the voices.

On his instructions, she had journeyed for nearly three days. Barely a teenager, she had never previously traveled more than five miles outside her village. Finally, cold and hungry, she stumbled into the ruins of an old stave church. After banishing a group of rats by waving her torch, she collapsed onto a patch of earth in a corner which still retained enough of its ceiling to provide protection from the elements.

The next morning, St. Michael directed her to a hidden staircase of stone which descended to a room, empty save for a single wooden box, the contents of which had shaken her to the core. Could it possibly be what she thought it was?

That worry was not enough for her to disregard the command of St. Michael, so she returned home with her discoveries, brushing aside questions from her father about where she had been. As time passed with no further reference to the box by the voice of the saint, the mystery only served to strengthen her faith in an all-knowing God. She made sure her secret was well hidden, and she waited.

When she was forced to leave home to escape her father's order to marry a local boy, she waited. When she convinced Robert de Baudricourt and then the King himself that God had charged her with leading the armies of France, she waited. After a glorious victory at Orleans, she waited. After ignoble defeat at Compiegne, she waited.

A lick of flame crackled next to her cheek, and her attention returned to her current predicament. She considered struggling against her restraints, but to what end? The Inquisitors were not in the habit of overlooking a detail such as securing their victim against escape. It seemed to Jehanne that she had spent almost the entire previous year bound to a stake or a wall.

Whenever she remembered her capture, the smell of death threatened to overwhelm her. The battle had left many men face down in the mud, and she had been thrown from her horse just before her army had retreated to the safety of the city. She had landed with her face buried in a putrid corpse. Jerking upright, she had heard a voice speaking the name the English Bishop had taken to calling her.

Joan.

She hated the name, but that was soon the least of her worries. She had waited in vain for the King to rescue her. Eventually St. Catherine had told her that she should not expect salvation from that quarter. Desperate to escape, she had managed to get to a window sixty feet above a dry moat and throw herself out. She sustained too many injuries to crawl further.

Finally St. Michael had spoken again last month, telling her that a trusted ally would appear to her within a week's time, and she should reveal her secret. Jehanne's faith had never wavered as much as it had in that moment. She had spent five months shackled to the wall of her cell, freed only to attend the sham of a trial that had so concerned the Inquisitors. More than once a guard had displayed an unhealthy interest in her, but pursuing that avenue further required unlocking her leg irons. The two scoundrels who had tried it lasted less than a minute each before Jehanne incapacitated them.

The idea that an ally would now appear seemed laughable. Only a true miracle from God could conjure up help in this purgatory on earth.

A week later, the miracle occurred.

Jehanne's evening meal failed to appear. She didn't miss the cold broth laced with an anemic dose of rotting vegetables, but her captors had been diligent about meals until now. In addition, she couldn't fail to notice the absence of the loud steps which usually accompanied a guard making hourly rounds. She did not know the reason for these deviations in routine, but she allowed her senses an extra level of focus on the sounds outside her door and single tiny casement.

The reason presented itself sometime near the apex of the darkness when her cell door slowly opened. So noiseless was the intruder that she almost missed it, but her eyes picked up a change in the shadow thrown by the half moon.

"Who is there?"

She made sure her challenge carried both volume and

authority. A hooded figure made its way toward her, finger raised into the folds of the cowl. Jehanne gasped as two gnarled hands lowered the hood.

"My child."

Jehanne's tears did not prevent her from responding to a man she recognized as her fondest ally. "Your Eminence. I am your servant."

A smile encompassed the entire face of Jacques Gelu, the Archbishop of Embrun. "You are wrong, young maid. I am yours."

"How did you get in?"

Gelu sighed. "Direct as always, I see. I shall endeavor to do the same. For many months, I have sought the King's ear regarding your fate. When I finally gained a real audience with him, I pointed out the disgrace of having the commander of great French victories languishing in an English gaol. Sadly, he would not be swayed."

Gelu reached out his hand and caressed Jehanne's face with a touch as gentle as an angel's wing. "He fears you, child." Wisps of gray hair trembled as Gelu shook his head. "You must allow an old man his secrets. It is enough to say that the hand of our almighty Father was involved."

Jehanne's gaze settled on his eyes, detecting nothing but affection. "As Your Eminence wishes. Why then have you come?"

"He will not say it aloud, but your power threatens him."

Jehanne rotated her palms upward inside her shackles. "My power? Tell me what power do you see now? All that I have comes from the Lord."

"It pains me to say it, but I think that is the point." Gelu's voice faded to a mere whisper. "There is even talk that the closing of the gate at Compiegne before you could get inside was done on his orders."

Jehanne felt her insides become steel, the way they did as she rode into battle. The tears which had accompanied her first sight of Gelu evaporated. Men had told her of the strength they saw when they observed her fair skin and dark hair mounted on a warhorse and riding toward bloodshed. *They have no idea of the strength that is possible with faith.*

Her voice remained level and unwavering. "So you came to tell me that I have been abandoned, and there is no hope."

"There is always hope if one trusts in our Savior."

"That is true, Your Eminence. Before you go, I have something to tell you."

He moved his face closer to hers. For three minutes, she spoke in low tones about the existence and location of the wooden box. She told him what he must do with it. When she was done, Gelu's face had begun to sag. He let out a slow breath.

"But if it is what you say, the faithful should…"

"No! My instructions come from St. Michael himself."

Gelu hesitated, his lips forming a retort, but he relented under Jehanne's stare. His eyes fell, his shoulders sagged, and he let out a slow breath.

"I cannot fathom the designs of our Lord. But it will be done."

"Thank you, Your Eminence. Now if you don't mind, I would like to be left alone."

She could tell that her abruptness shocked him, but her decision was made. She knew what she had to do, and she knew how it would end.

She heard a gasp, and it took a second before she realized that it had escaped her own lips. The first real pain from the flames had shattered her remembrance. She cast her eyes over the crowd, full of faces more flush from the bloodlust than the heat. She closed them again quickly, knowing that she would never gaze on anything again in the earthly realm.

Jehanne prayed that the growing pain would end quickly. St. Michael came to her then, and she felt the pain lessen enough that she considered opening her eyes again to see if the fire had been doused. But a deeper part of her knew that she was now in the hands of the angels. She focused on one final prayer.

Please, Lord, protect the box. Whatever it holds is your creation. Let it be one day found by a man whose imperfection is not so great as to render him incapable of using it as you desire.

November 7, 1751
Barbados

Washington knew the signal tower was vulnerable the moment he saw it. The British commander sounded proud of the structure, boasting of its height and solid construction. Situated behind the walls of St. Ann's Fort and within easy sight of the coast, the tower enabled communication with naval and land forces alike.

But it was still a weak point. At age nineteen, Washington had already taken a keen interest in military matters. He knew that heavy cannons could easily fire over the walls and destroy the signal tower. High ground like that was a wonderful thing in war, but only if it was defensible. A single light artillery weapon at the top would protect it about as effectively as a child's wooden rifle.

Washington had arrived in Barbados with his brother, Lawrence, less than a week earlier. Lawrence was quite ill with tuberculosis, and the tropical climate of the island would restore his health more effectively than a damp Virginia winter. So far the humidity had served only to depress his brother's energy levels, but Washington still held out hope. In the meantime, he had undertaken to learn as much as he could about the local military structures.

The British were delighted to indulge the young man. Everyone knew that war between Britain and France was coming, and North America promised to play a leading role. A colonial well-versed in proper British military theory would be valuable indeed. Washington approached his research with the same methodical care that he approached everything else in his life. He could see plenty of holes, but he didn't see any point in offending his hosts.

"Quite an impressive structure. How many men are

generally stationed there?"

The colonel twirled the handlebars of his mustache, a carefully manicured fixture of white facial hair which contrasted with jowls flush from some combination of alcohol and the Caribbean sun. "Two under normal circumstances. We rarely see much excitement, but additional runners would be made available if needed. I daresay a single man to manage a fire is sufficient."

Washington only nodded, taking one final look as the colonel led the way toward the ocean-facing ramparts. The tower was made of gray stone, reaching several dozen feet into the cloudless sky. Stout rungs extended from one sheer wall. An ascent to the top would be easy in calm times, but a man not familiar with them could expect to risk a nasty fall if forced to climb at top speed. Possibly there was enough space at the top for three or four men, but firing even a single cannon in those tight quarters would create some of the same risks ships faced with sub-deck guns. If Washington ever needed to commission a tower such as this one, he'd make a lot of improvements.

The rest of the tour proceeded without any incident of note. Upon return to the house he had secured for his brother's convalescence, he found his brother mentally alert but physically worsened. Washington steadied himself before speaking to the shell of a man who had once been a vigorous older sibling.

"You're not looking well, Lawrence."

A cough preceded the reply. "Never one to dance around the truth, are you Georgie? I know perfectly well that I'm closer to visiting our Lord than I was yesterday."

"Technically the same is true of all of us."

"I suppose it is. Tell me, are you still unable to call me anything but Lawrence? I must confess that the formality has worn thin as I ponder my mortality."

Washington opened his mouth and then closed it. What was the point of a person's given name if not to be used for address? He could handle analyzing military matters or farming methods, but he had not yet mastered dealing with those close to him. "Do you need anything? I have some matters to attend to after our evening meal."

Lawrence Washington's lids drooped. "No, brother, I need nothing you can give me. But I would have you stay with me for a time. Tell me of your doings in the larger world that I fear I shall never experience again."

Later that evening, Washington headed back to St. Ann's Fort. He wasn't entirely sure it was a good idea, but he knew he could learn a lot more about how a military force conducted business by observing them outside of a scheduled tour. Despite his interest in fortifications and structures, he knew that an army's fortunes owed much to the commitment level of its men. Sometimes such things could be learned only in a practical way. Tonight he would attempt a clandestine breach of the fort's outer walls.

Most who knew him would have expressed surprise at such a seemingly rash action. Washington, however, had reasoned carefully. Every member of the garrison had seen him during his visit earlier in the day, so he would be familiar to nearly anyone who would challenge him. If they caught him, the British would be reluctant to alienate someone so well-connected among the American colonists whose aid they would soon need. And the biggest reason Washington felt his planned incursion was a worthy risk derived from his initial assessment of the fort and its commander: he suspected that their sense of superiority underestimated the threat from pirates, natives, and any other potential attackers.

The night was one for which Noah would have found himself well-prepared. Washington had scarcely spurred his mount before the skies opened up. He had seen the thunderheads building and attired himself appropriately, but that proved small consolation as the dampness managed to target every weakness in his layer of oilskin. He mused that the difficult conditions would tell him more about the British than he otherwise could have gleaned. At least the tropical heat ensured no danger from a chill.

Given the conditions, the massive quarter horse could

only move at a pace that a slow man might manage on foot, but eventually Washington arrived near the outside gate of the fort. He dismounted, secured the beast, and made his way closer without a lantern. A tree defoliated by the hurricanes which regularly buffeted the island provided a thick enough trunk to conceal him.

The lanterns adorning the area around the gate were visible through the torrent only as fuzzy splotches of light. He spotted a single guard standing in place, holding a lantern even more anemic than the fixed ones. For the next thirty minutes, Washington watched in silence. The only interruption he witnessed was another guard approaching from along the fortified walls, clearly finishing some sort of patrol. The new arrival took up the static position and the initial guard began trudging back in the direction from which the newcomer had come. Washington felt some compassion for the man, who even through the dark and rain gave the impression of hopelessness.

Were he actually planning an incursion into enemy territory, Washington would not have proceeded. He didn't know if there were more guards. He didn't have a full idea of what lay on the seaward side of the fort. But he strongly suspected he had seen all he needed to see, so after a moment, he began moving in the same direction as the departing guard. He remained forty yards away from the wall, feeling exposed.

Soon enough, the gate was out of sight. He stopped after another fifty yards, moving quickly toward the wall. One thing the British had done correctly was to keep the area surrounding the walls of the fort clear of significant vegetation aside from scrub no more than eighteen inches tall. Ironically, he would be less exposed right up against the fort itself than at any point approaching it.

He never reached the wall. A cough from behind him stopped him in his tracks after only a few steps. He whirled, taking less than a second to weigh the pros and cons of drawing his pistol. He decided against it.

He saw nothing. He felt exposed, wishing for a lantern

but knowing he had made the right decision in proceeding without one. Minutes passed, and he allowed his eyes to adjust fully to the darkness. He thought he could make out a shape in the dark, not right in front of him but close enough for him to pick it up. Then again, it could be his mind playing tricks on him after staring at nothing for so long.

Then he heard the cough again, and he decided to press the issue. "Show yourself."

Hearing no response, he persisted. "I am no enemy if that's what you're concerned about."

After a heartbeat, a phlegmy explosion pierced the night, as if a cannon were fired several times under water. The shape in the dark appeared again, this time with more substance and moving toward him. He reached for his pistol. The man – for by now it was clear that the shape was human – came closer. Then he collapsed at Washington's feet.

"Enemy or friend, none of that will be my concern for much longer."

The voice was a low and raspy whisper, heaving with effort. A light appeared, and Washington saw a lantern on the ground with a set of gnarled fingers wrapped around the handle. The man must have kept it shielded until this moment. This man could not be part of the garrison, and Washington began to wonder if the light would attract the attention of the guards. He had been prepared for the possibility of being captured inside the fort, so he wouldn't spend any time worrying about discovery fifty yards away.

"Who are you?" Washington heard his own voice as a hard challenge, but this unaccustomed situation had removed some of the filter he generally applied to his direct nature.

Another series of coughs preceded the answer, this one more distressed than the prior. "I shouldn't tell you. It is supposed to be a secret. It's been a secret for over three decades. But I am an old man, and I may not make it through the night. My name is Israel Hands."

Washington waited.

"I see that name means nothing to you. That is no surprise, as my name has meant nothing to anyone since before you were born. But perhaps you have heard of the ship I commanded. It was called the *Adventure*."

A bubble of recognition bounced in Washington's brain, but it didn't settle anywhere. "I am sorry, sir, but I'm not familiar with that vessel,"

Hands held up the lantern and squinted. "Ah yes, you are indeed a young man. No doubt you've heard of the sister ship of the *Adventure*. That was originally called *La Concorde*, but you would know it as the *Queen Anne's Revenge*."

Washington did know the ship, and his hand went to his pistol again. The next sound that came from Hands' mouth was either a cough or a laugh. "Put away your pistol. I am no threat to anyone, least of all a man from Virginia."

Washington's eyes went wide, and his hand stayed put. "You know of me?"

This time, the laugh was more pronounced. "I do not. But I have an ear for accents, and I spent much time in Virginia. I was nearly hanged there."

"From what you've said so far, that is not surprising."

"Don't be so quick to judge, young sir When you hear the full story, you will..." Hands began coughing again, expelling red gobs large enough to be seen even by dull lantern light in the rain. He collapsed onto his side and drew his knees to his chest, his chest heaving with every cough.

Washington knew some people found him cold, but he was not without compassion. He dropped to his knees and put a hand on the man's forehead. The heat radiated even before their flesh touched. Washington kept his hand there until the coughing subsided.

Hands didn't move from a near-fetal position, but he spoke again. "I have come so close, but I have failed. Listen if you will about one of the greatest treasures known to God and man. I was pardoned over three decades ago when I was but a step from the gallows. Since then I have dedicated myself to finding the treasure. I'm sure you heard rumors about it and dismissed them as the fantasies of the weak-minded. I spent many years without a single clue, but I finally retraced our steps to this island. To be honest, I held out little hope."

"The island has given me two things. The first is the location of the journal. Yesterday I tracked down Cyrus Vane, a sailor on the *Revenge,* one hell of a fighter and a scoundrel. With a tongue loosened by rum, he told me of the journal."

Washington felt his pulse quicken. Hands had referenced the very thing which had piqued his own interest. Washington believed in God in the same way many rational men of his standing did: as a distant entity whose existence was certain but whose role in day to day life was largely irrelevant. For the first time in his life, he wondered if he had received a sign from God.

"What was the other thing the island gave you?"

Hands still had not moved, but his voice was clear enough. "The other thing the island gave me was smallpox. Sometimes I wonder if our Lord has a sense of humor."

Another coughing fit began, and Washington stood quickly. Smallpox was not common in Virginia, and he had never been exposed. But he'd heard enough of its horrors to experience fear at seeing an infected man lying before him. In fact, it took most of his willpower not to back away.

"Why are you telling me this?"

"The secret can't die with me. The treasure, it is so much more than I believed…"

What is in the journal? And what is the treasure?"

Hands raised a single finger and spoke in wracked breaths. "Cayman Brac… beneath the eagle…"

Another cough, wet and weak, and Hands breathed no more.

ONE

Dane Maddock had always wondered whether a single finger could support one hundred and ninety pounds of Navy SEAL. Clinging to the edge of a rock face fifty feet above the ground, he suspected he was about to find out.

His left hand was extended as far as possible with a solid hold. His left foot and right foot each rested in the slightest of indentations, providing mostly friction instead of actually carrying his weight. As climbing positions went, it was almost comfortable, and Maddock could have remained there almost indefinitely. The problem was where to go next.

He ran his right hand along the rock at the furthest extent of his reach, confirming what he already knew. Smooth as a baby's bottom except for one protrusion. A protrusion which provided room for a single finger.

"Sucks being such a little guy, huh, Maddock?"

Maddock scowled. Bones was six and a half feet of muscled Native American, with a wingspan that would make a condor feel inadequate. Maddock could claim six feet only if he let his hair grow for a few months and used a lot of gel.

They had gone through SEAL training together, and at first, Maddock had despised the big man. Bones was forever making light of serious situations and bucking authority. They'd even come to blows in one memorable incident. But they'd shared a number of harrowing adventures recently, and Maddock now appreciated the skill and courage which accompanied the levity. There was no better man to have at your side when things got hairy.

After discovering a mutual interest in climbing, they'd planned this trip to Virginia to explore some of the challenging routes in the area. This was actually the first time they'd climbed together, and the trash talking before the climb had escalated to playground basketball levels. Maddock was ten feet above Bones; if he could just get six feet to his right, he would have a pretty clear path for the final twenty feet. Bones was clearly trying to slow him down.

"Seems to me that this little guy is already out of your reach."

"It just looks that way, dude. There's only one direction you can go, and it ain't toward the sky."

Maddock gritted his teeth. He could grab the tiny hold with a finger, release his other limbs and swing...and he'd still only be halfway there. He had an anchor planted fifteen feet down, but falling thirty feet before it caught and bounced him off the cliff was not high on his bucket list. The thing was, any other option except trying this move would mean Bones overtaking him.

Maddock was not going to let that happen. He flexed his right index finger, took a deep breath, and curled the finger around the minuscule hold.

As he unweighted his left side, the grip felt solid. His full weight was not on the finger yet, and before that could happen he whipped his left hand across. Then he made the second-hardest move of the sequence, removing his right finger so he was floating free for a fraction of a second before his left finger took its place. That's where he made his first mistake.

Instead of his left index finger supporting him, his left middle finger was doing the job. A small wave of panic shot through him, but the part of him which had survived SEAL training took over and smashed the panic into submission. With hardly any sense of actually holding onto the face, he thrust his right hand and foot toward solid holds he had spied before beginning the move.

Both hand and foot successfully found their targets, but his left finger slipped before his right side was fully secure. His left side swung out into the air, like a door opening on its hinges. As he struggled to strengthen his remaining holds, Maddock began to brace himself for the inevitable fall.

The fall never came. Somehow he stabilized himself and wound up hugging the face again. His breathing took the better part of a minute to return to normal, whether from the panic or the exertion he couldn't be sure. He glanced down at Bones.

"No smartass remarks this time?"

Bones' grin was easily visible below him. "Maddock, that was one of the dumbest moves I have ever seen. I told you hanging around with me was going to rub off on you."

"I won't be hanging around much longer. I'll see you at the top."

Five minutes later he gained the ledge at the summit, the route relatively easy compared to what had come before. He sat taking in the beauty of the forested Blue Ridge Mountains. When Bones made his way onto the ledge, Maddock looked at his watch.

"What kept you?"

"I took my time. Didn't want to make you feel bad about your climbing skills after what I just saw. But seriously, Dude, whose ass did you pull that move out of? Admit it, you only did it because it allowed you to give me the finger when I couldn't pound you for it."

Maddock shook his head, and the two friends exchanged an intense stare.

Bones said, "I'll deny I ever said this, but...nice move, man."

"Deny you ever said what?"

"Not as dumb as you look."

A shrill ring cut through the heavy summer air. Maddock flinched before remembering that his cell phone was tucked in the tiny pack strapped close to his back. Maddock had resisted getting a cell phone for a long time, but once or twice Bones' device had come in very handy. His friend Jimmy Letson said that within a decade phones would be more powerful than the current personal computers. Maddock only cared that he could make and receive a call, which apparently was possible in the middle of nowhere.

"If that's Maxie, don't answer it. The good old commander lives to screw up our time off. Remember that time he sent us on a week of hell for a super-secret mission that was only supposed to take two days?"

"Which time?"

Bones smirked. "You see my point."

"It could be Melissa." Not many people had Maddock's number, but his girlfriend, Melissa Moore, did. They had first met in Boston the previous year, and after some long distance correspondence and several visits to determine if they really wanted to pursue a relationship, they both acknowledged that they had fallen hard.

Bones sighed. "How someone with your skills can be so thoroughly whipped is beyond me. Don't say I didn't warn you. How about you pretend to lose the connection if it's Maxie."

Maddock extracted the phone from his pack. Why have the thing if he wasn't going to answer it. It *could* be their commanding officer, but he doubted it.

"Hello?"

The familiar voice came on the phone, but it contained tension he had never heard before. "Dane, Thank God you're there. I need you."

Rarely had words triggered such a rush of adrenaline. Melissa was in trouble. Maddock had always been the type who would help anyone in trouble, even help the occasional little old lady across the street. So when the woman he cared about most in the world called for help, an army couldn't have prevented him from rushing to her side.

His mind also registered one of the many things he appreciated about Melissa – her focus and lack of drama. Eight words were all she needed.

"Where are you?"

"Work."

He looked at his watch. "I can be there in an hour. Are you hurt? Are you in immediate danger? Do you need me to call someone?"

"No, no, I'm fine. The police will be here any minute. But Sarah was attacked and… well, it was really weird and I don't think the cops are up to this sort of thing."

Maddock felt a tingling sensation in his neck, one he

had by now learned never to ignore. It happened when something important was imminent. Usually something involving bad guys trying to put one over on good guys. He hated that. "Hold on."

Melissa worked at Mt. Vernon during the summer, not exactly a terrorist target or even any kind of sensitive location. Sarah Abrams was her boss, a curator/administrator in charge of the interns. Maddock looked at Bones and relayed her words.

Bones whistled. "Mysterious goings on with something related to George Washington? Are you getting that same feeling deep in your bowels that I am?"

"That's more detail than I ever need about your digestive tract, Bones, but yeah we're on the same page."

Melissa's voice came over the phone which was still attached to Maddock's ear. "Are you still there?"

"Yeah, honey, I'm still here. One hour, maybe less."

"Aren't you eighty miles away?"

"Yep, on a ledge seventy-five feet off the ground. I'm gonna let Bones drive."

"Bones driving? So either you'll be here in forty-five minutes or you'll die in a fiery crash. Lovely."

"I heard that," Bones called.

Melissa managed a laugh. "I'm glad you're bringing him along. My spidey senses are on high alert."

"That makes three of us. Be there as soon as we can." He hung up before she could begin their normal sappy goodbye. She'd understand.

Bones raised his eyebrows. "You're gonna *let* me drive? I think you have it backward, kemosabe. I'm the one who sometimes lets you drive."

"So the fact that the rental car company refused to rent to you after what happened last time has no bearing on the topic?"

"None whatsoever. I'm the victim of a smear campaign."

"Bones, you're driving. Let's get an anchor in up here and take the express elevator down."

Within three minutes, they'd anchored the hundred foot rope on the ledge and slid down it without pause. Maddock hated to lose a good rope, but with Melissa possibly at risk he didn't give it a second thought. They reached the rented Crown Victoria a minute later, and Bones was pulling out even before Maddock had the door closed.

Once on the highway, Bones pushed the pedal to the floor. "We have reached our cruising speed of one hundred and five miles an hour. You are now free to watch carefully for the fuzz."

"At this speed, we'll be by them before we even see them."

Bones shrugged. "Hey, maybe they won't see us."

"Bones, we're speeding, we're not invisible."

"Speak for yourself. My people invented stealth."

"Right, the proud Cherokee tradition of pushing an eight-cylinder engine to its limits. Look if we see cops, we're not stopping."

Bones took his eyes off the road for just a moment to glance at Maddock. "Wow, first that crazy move on the rock and now this. What's going on?"

"I have no idea, Bones."

Maddock turned his gaze to the windshield, as if looking toward their destination could make it appear more quickly. Almost to himself, he mumbled a few words.

"Whatever it is, I just hope we're not too late."

TWO

Fifty-seven minutes after he hung up the phone, they skidded to a halt in the Mount Vernon parking lot. Maddock leaped out of the car and hit the ground at a near run, stopping only to pay their admission fee before hurrying up the hill toward the main building.

Mount Vernon stood atop a long, gently sloping hill. The sun gleamed on its white boards, red roof, and high cupola. Outbuildings, their walls and roofs matching in color, flanked a drive that ended in a roundabout in front of the main door.

Melissa waited outside the door. She embraced him and buried her head in his shoulder. He could feel the muscles in her shoulders and upper back move as she breathed deeply. He just held on.

The moment passed quickly as she pulled away and looked him in the eyes.

He could stare at that delicate face and green eyes forever, and he never could resist the urge to run his fingers through her fine brown hair. Sometimes he wondered...

"Did you hear what I said?"

He realized Melissa had been speaking and he snapped himself back into focus. He saw no trace of tears or weakness, just focus and a touch of exasperation.

"Sorry, I was busy admiring your lovely face. What did you say?"

"I said you need to come with me right now. The police are still interviewing Sarah in one of the servant's buildings, and I want to show you something before they decide to seal the place off."

He and Bones followed her through the main door. They passed beneath the winding staircase that led up to the second floor and stepped out into the central passage, a wood-paneled entryway with two doors on either side, leading to different parts of the house, and a larger door directly ahead which opened onto terrace, the iconic covered porch that looked down onto the Potomac. On the wall to their right hung a glass case which held a large iron key. Nothing seemed unusual about the room except perhaps the presence of half a dozen muddy footprints.

Bones scanned the room. "What's the problem? You want us to beat up the janitorial squad?"

Melissa rolled her eyes. "Don't pull that ignorant crap on me, *Uriah*. I know you better than that. The problem is that someone messed with the Bastille Key." She pointed to the key in the glass case.

Bones appealed to Maddock. "Dude, she called me Uriah. I've killed men for less."

Maddock ignored him. "What's this Bastille Key?"

"It's a key to the famous French prison. It was a gift to George Washington from Marquis de Lafayette back in 1790."

Maddock walked over to the display. "Looks fine to me."

She sighed. "The key itself is fine. But see how those footprints are darkest right by the case? When I saw that, I took a closer look. Reach your hand under the case."

"Won't that set off the alarm?"

She shook her head. "We turned the alarms off in this building when the police arrived."

Maddock's fingers immediately discovered some sort of hinge mechanism not visible from a normal view. He squatted down and examined it. The lock showed clear signs of forced entry and was now held in place with a single nail through the hasps.

"Did they take or damage anything?"

"Not as far as I can tell. But take a look at that bit of green stuff at the bottom of the case."

This time, Bones also leaned over to get a better view. Maddock pulled his fingers away with a small bit of the substance on his fingers. It felt like...

"Wax." Bones exclaimed. "So we know they were after the key."

Maddock frowned. "How do we know that?"

Bones shook his head. "Sheesh, you need to get with the program. The wax means——."

He stopped and looked at Melissa. "Do you want to tell him or should I?"

Melissa shrugged. "I don't actually know what the deal is. I just thought it was suspicious."

"Fair enough," Bones said. "Lucky for you two I have a checkered past. The wax tells us they're making a copy of the key."

Voices sounded at the entryway and two police detectives entered, escorting Sarah Abrams. Bones and Maddock had met the forty-something curator two days earlier when they had arrived from their San Diego training base. Despite weighing less than a hundred pounds at five-four or five-five, she had bubbled with energy, her blond locks dancing as she gave them a rush tour of some Mount Vernon highlights. Now Abrams looked pale, her eyes focused in the distance despite standing and shaking hands with one of two detectives in the room.

The other detective entered. He stood a couple inches taller than Maddock, with light brown skin and short, black hair. He cast a solid figure despite some extra pounds around the middle. His brown eyes scanned the doorway and his hand moved slowly about three inches toward the inside of his jacket. Most people would have failed to notice this, but Maddock knew the man was preparing for the possibility of having to draw a weapon. He made sure his hands were clearly visible and at his sides.

The officer stopped the motion toward his jacket and extended his hand instead.

"Detective Dwayne Ramos. You must be Dane Maddock." He spoke with a slow, southern drawl, unusual for the DC area.

Maddock's eyes must have betrayed his surprise at hearing his name, because Ramos chuckled as he took the offered hand. "Your little lady said y'all would be coming along to keep an eye on her. I thought she was spinning a yarn about Mr. Bonebrake here, but if anything she didn't rightly do him justice."

Bones laughed. "Story of my life. Was it my charm or my good looks that caught you off guard?"

Ramos narrowed his eyes for a moment before a grin returned. "She mentioned your height, but mostly she warned me about your mouth."

Melissa avoided the ensuing glare from Bones and managed to keep a straight face. "What can you tell us, Detective?"

"Nothing you don't already know, I'm sorry to say. She was hit from behind and didn't get a good look at her attacker. We'll be taking her to Inovo just to get her checked out."

"Inovo?" Maddock asked?

"Hospital a few miles away in Alexandria. In the meantime, Ms. Moore, we need to get your statement."

"No problem, but I'm following you to Inovo afterward. Sarah needs to have someone with her."

Ramos looked at Bones and Maddock.

"SEALs, right?"

Maddock nodded.

"I did four years as a squid myself before I landed at Mt. Vernon P.D. You boys know I can't have you in here for the interview?"

Maddock frowned. "I suspected that."

Ramos' gaze drifted to the Bastille key and his eyes widened. "I didn't realize this is the room where the…" He turned to his partner. "Get those idiots outside to seal off this room." He turned back to Melissa and forced a smile. "I'm sorry about that. This room should have been sealed off immediately. When it wasn't taped off, I assume the key was in another location. Let's talk about somewhere else. How about the study?"

Maddock jumped in. "I'm not sure that's a good idea, Detective."

For the first time, Ramos showed confusion. "Why is that?"

Maddock didn't answer. Instead he strode through the small bedchamber that lay between the central passage and the study, stopping at the study door.

"This partial print looks like it's a match for the ones near the Bastille key." He pointed to a crescent shaped section of a heel print.

Ramos wasted no time in shouldering past Maddock and ordering everyone to stay out of the study. Maddock, Bones, and Melissa stood just outside the door, watching as the detective scanned the floor for more prints and then looked all around.

"Ms. Moore, Ms. Abrams," he finally said, "will you please come in here? And be careful not to disturb the footprint."

Melissa stepped inside, Maddock keeping his eyes trained on her, followed by Sarah. Something about Ramos put him on the defensive.

"You are more familiar with this room than I am. Do you see anything out of sorts?"

Melissa and Sarah looked around.

"The books inside the case have been disturbed," Sarah said. "See how some have been pulled out and not pushed all the way back in? They're not usually like that."

Ramos nodded. "We'll have to fingerprint the case. Anything else?"

Melissa turned in a slow circle, paused, and frowned. "The portrait of Washington is different." She pointed to a painting on the wall. Washington sat in a wooden chair, left hand on his thigh, looking off to the side.

"What do you mean? Someone moved it?"

She frowned and tapped her pursed lips, a habit Maddock found extremely attractive.

"I can't say for sure. There's just something different about it. Sorry, that's all I can say."

"All right." Ramos turned to Maddock and Bones. "How about you gentlemen clear out entirely? Lord knows what else our team has missed." He turned his back, Maddock and Bones already forgotten.

"These guys are clueless," Bones whispered.

"Why? Because they missed something?"

"That wasn't all they missed. Buy me a cup of coffee and I'll tell you all about it."

THREE

"Dude, you should have seen the look on that cop's face."
Bones' soft laugh sounded like a thunderclap in the quiet
Mount Vernon snack bar.

"Bones, I was standing right there. I *did* see the look on
his face. In his defense, he was focusing on the victim
instead of the property crime." He took a sip of his coffee
and grimaced. It was like drinking hot water filtered through
potting soil. "So," he said, setting his cup down on the table,
"what were you going to tell me?"

"These guys are half-assing it. I saw another print
leading up the stairs and more on the piazza."

"Why didn't you say anything to them?"

Bones shrugged. "Screw 'em. If they're paying any sort
of attention they'll find them. The point is, whoever was
here wanted more than a copy of the Bastille key."

"Don't try to tell them that." Melissa slid into a chair in
between them. "They're not finished looking around, but
Ramos seems to think it's no big deal."

"How does he figure that?" Maddock asked.

"The guy who grabbed Sarah kept asking, 'Where is the
journal?' She had no idea what he was talking about. I
mean, Washington kept a journal while he was in the British
army, but it's not lost or anything. Heck, you can find scans
of it online"

"So he was looking for some other journal," Bones said.

"Which explains why the books in the study had been
disturbed," Maddock added.

Melissa nodded. "Ramos thinks it was a black market
antiquities dealer."

"One who shows up in the middle of the day?" Bones
gave a slow shake of his head. "Give me a freaking break."

"And what about the Bastille key?" Maddock asked.

"Ramos says the guy probably wants to sell copies to
unsuspecting buyers."

Maddock buried his face in his hands. "Seriously? Why wouldn't he just steal the key?"

"An alarm goes off if it's removed from the case. He'd have likely been caught. Ramos figures the guy slipped in between tours, made a quick casting of the key, and then poked around the study. When he heard Sarah coming, he panicked."

"How does he explain the footprints leading up the stairs?" Bones asked. "Or did he even find them?"

"He found a couple on the stairs but nothing else, and everything upstairs appears normal, at least, *according to Sarah.*"

"You sound like you're not too happy with her," Maddock said.

"She treated me like an idiot. I swear there's something about the portrait in the study, but she dismissed me out of hand. After that, everyone treated me like I'm a buffoon." She reached out and took Maddock's hand. "I don't think Ramos is taking this seriously. What if this guy comes back?"

Maddock checked his watch. It was almost closing time. "How about Bones and I come back for some late night detective work?"

"Break into Mount Vernon? Oh hell yes." Bones pounded his fist on the table, startling an elderly couple seated two tables away.

"A little louder next time," Maddock said. "I don't think they heard you in DC."

"Bite me, Maddock."

"The two of you?" Melissa's eyebrows sprang up. "I'm the one who can get you in here, disable the alarms, and turn off the security cameras. I'm the one who will notice if something's out of sorts. You're not leaving me out of this."

"Wait a minute," Bones said, "how do you know how to do all that stuff?"

"I like to learn things, and the head of security has a thing for me."

Maddock sat up a little straighter.

"Don't worry. Just a little harmless flirting. I did the same thing with the head archivist, and now I know the passcode to the secure area."

"Where did you find this chick, Maddock?" Bones smiled in approval.

"Hey, I was straight-laced when I met you." She blushed and glanced away. "Okay, that's a lie, but these adventures you've been telling me about have brought out my... devious side." She grinned at Maddock. "Admit it. Aren't you happy to have me at your disposal?"

A cool breeze rolled up off the Potomac, and Melissa gave a little shudder and pressed her body against Maddock.

"I don't know if I'm cold or just nervous," she whispered.

Maddock wrapped his arms around her and gave her a squeeze. "You're doing great. If it weren't for you, we'd have probably set off an alarm or two."

"Hey," Bones said, "a little more confidence in my burglary abilities, if you please. I could have gotten us in."

"Sure you could have," Melissa said, "but isn't this way easier?" She unlocked the veranda door, stepped inside, and quickly disabled the alarm.

"Where do you want to start?" Bones whispered.

"The study. I want another look at the Washington portrait."

They moved quickly to the study, with only faint security lights and the dull moonlight shining through the windows to light their way. Once inside the study, Melissa took out a small hardbound book and a penlight. "There's a shot of the study in here. It shows the painting." She shone the light on the page and they spent a few seconds absorbing it, then she turned the light on the painting. "See anything different?"

Bones shrugged. "His package is smaller? Bigger?"

Melissa let out an exasperated sigh.

"Let's see the picture again," Maddock said.

Melissa shone the light on the image and it clicked into

place.

"Look at Washington's left hand," Maddock said.

"He's holding a book," Bones said.

"Now look at the painting on the wall."

Melissa turned her light to the portrait and gasped. "The book's gone."

"What the hell?" Bones asked. "He switched out the paintings? What for?"

"I'll bet that's the journal he's looking for. He's just removing a visual reminder of its existence. Think about it. It's so subtle that Sarah didn't even notice."

"The painting's small," Bones agreed. "It would be a pain, but a big guy could smuggle it in or out under his jacket."

Maddock ran a hand through his hair. "So he switched the real painting for a fake one, and he clearly intends to make a fake Bastille key. This is weird."

They made a quick inspection of the room, but nothing else caught Melissa's eye, so they proceeded to the stairs. The police had noticed only a couple of footprints, but Bones' sharp eye was far superior. He noted scuffs and tiny bits of dirt that the police had missed. The big Cherokee quickly led them into a second-floor bedroom.

"This is the Lafayette Bedchamber," Melissa said. "Marquis de Lafayette was like a son to Washington, and this was where he stayed on his visits."

Maddock shone his light around the room, its beam playing off the canopy bed, armchairs, washstand, and fireplace, eventually landing on a gold-framed portrait of the Marquis himself.

"What did he want in here?" Melissa asked.

"Looks like…" Bones moved slowly across the carpeted floor, following a trail only he could see, "he stopped right in front of this painting." Bones shone his light on the wall around the painting. "I think he took it down. You can see a gold smudge where he banged the frame against the wall."

"You think he switched this one too?" Melissa asked.

Maddock shook his head. "Too big. Let's take a closer

look."

He slipped on a pair of gloves, took the painting down, and laid it face-down on the bed. "I wonder..." He worked the thin wooden backing out of the frame and pulled it free. Just as he had suspected, it was a false backing. He flipped it over and whistled in surprise.

"There was something here."

In the center of the backing were eight ragged corners of yellowed paper.

"Somebody glued pages from...something in here," Bones said.

"And our friend found them and tore them free." Maddock hung the painting back up. "The plot thickens."

"I guess we've hit a dead end," Melissa said.

"Not necessarily. We can research the journal, and also see if we can find out what might have been hidden in this portrait."

"As long as we're here, we might as well follow the footprints out on the piazza," Bones said. "Maybe he went somewhere else while he was here."

Outside, Bones quickly pointed out a footprint that he claimed matched those of the intruder.

"The guy was coming this way when he left this print, so I guess we'll be retracing his steps."

Maddock could scarcely make out the print in the soft earth, but he trusted Bones. He and Melissa followed his friend as Bones followed the tracks around the main house, past the outbuildings, and along the trees that lined the front lawn. Halfway down, they cut across the greenspace and picked up the trail again among the trees on the opposite side.

"He was clearly trying to keep out of sight," Maddock said.

"Like it was necessary," Bones said. "There's hardly any security in this place."

They cut through a series of gardens, crossed a wide walkway, and soon found themselves staring at a gray, metal door at the back of the Mount Vernon Museum. Bones took out his Maglite and gave it a close inspection.

"Do you want me to pick the lock or let Melissa handle it?"

"Get out of the way." Melissa slipped past Bones, tapped in a code on the keypad, and, pushed the door open.

Maddock stepped inside and flicked on his flashlight, revealing a storage room filled with row upon row of shelves. They followed the footprints on the floor, found where they stopped, inspected the boxes in this area.

"There's a gap here," he said, shining his light on an empty space. "Do you have any idea what was here?"

"As matter of fact, I do. I was just in here the other day."

"Hooking up with someone?" Maddock asked.

Melissa ignored him. "A museum in Boston came across some artifacts from a visit Washington made there in 1791. They were mixed in with items belonging to Sam Adams and were only recently identified. The archivist was just inventorying it."

Bones and Maddock exchanged a meaningful look. They knew something about Washington's 1791 visit to Boston that few others knew, and even fewer would believe.

Melissa looked around. "There it is." She pointed to a single box on the top shelf. "The guy put it back in the wrong place. Must have been in a hurry."

Bones took it down and handed it to her. She opened it, took out a sheet of paper containing an itemized list of the contents, and compared it to what was in the box.

"There's one item missing. A letter to Lafayette that was never mailed."

"A deathbed letter to his surrogate son," Bones said.

"What do you mean by deathbed?" Melissa asked, replacing the box.

Just then the lights switched on and a voice came from near the door. "Hands in the air, Bonebrake. Maddock, I know you're in here. This is Detective Ramos. Speak up to acknowledge that you heard me."

"Is there another way out of here?" Maddock mouthed

to Melissa.

She shook her head.

"Anywhere you can hide?"

She nodded.

"Go."

Melissa slunk away, vanishing behind the rows of shelves.

Anger laced Ramos' next words. "You boys may think I'm just some local hick, but you'd do well to think again. There's no other way out of here and I called for backup as soon as I saw y'all sneakin' in. Be a shame if you was roughed up when we take you into custody."

Maddock prayed Bones could resist that kind of provocation. He closed his eyes and waited for his friend to respond to the challenge. Thankfully, Bones kept his silence.

"I'm getting tired of waiting. You got five seconds to show yourself before I start sending bullets your way."

Maddock remained silent. Ramos didn't know they were there, and if he wanted to search for them, he'd have to pick a side of the room to check out first. Left or right? If he chose badly, they might be able to outflank him.

Five seconds passed, and Maddock heard a light scraping of footsteps. They weren't loud enough for him to determine the direction in which Ramos was moving. Maddock grabbed a book from the shelf next to him and tossed it over a shelving unit toward the doorway.

The thud of it striking the ground sounded out of proportion to the size of the tome. He half expected the detective to fire a shot in that direction, but the man wasn't falling for it. Maddock wanted to do something else besides just stand there, but he knew that the worst thing he could do was to move without a definite plan. So he crouched near the end of an aisle where he was hidden by shadows but still had freedom to move quickly if needed.

Then he heard the faintest of whispers.

"Dominos."

Maddock had to hand it to his friend. Bones' plan would likely create the diversion they needed to escape. Standing about ten feet apart, they each shoved hard on one of the shelving units. The groaning of metal preceded the toppling of the seven-foot-high structure. It bridged the four feet of aisle on the other side and then crashed into the next unit.

As that unit started to fall, Maddock and Bones bolted for the door. Before reaching it, they heard a cry of surprise, and Maddock hoped that Ramos had been struck by one of the falling shelves. He fumbled with the door handle before realizing that Ramos had locked it from the inside. The man definitely wasn't dumb. He quickly unlocked it and he and Bones stepped out into a dimly lit corridor.

And found themselves face to face with three uniformed police officers with guns drawn and pointing at the door.

"I'm telling you, you've got the wrong guys." Bones tried to slap the table with his hands, but the manacles allowed him only a couple inches of leverage.

Detective Ramos held a disposable ice pack over a bruise just under his right eye, which had turned a dark purple in the two hours since an unidentified object from the collapsing shelf had struck him. His expression did not convey enjoyment. On the plus side, he hadn't said a word about Melissa, which indicated the detective had no clue about the role she'd played.

"Bonebrake, I imagine you think you're funny. We got you boys dead to rights breaking into one of our most sacred landmarks, not to mention destruction of private property and assaulting a police officer. The courts round these here parts don't take kindly to that sort of thing, and given the judicial backlog, y'all could be our guests here for quite some time. So, how 'bout we try again and you tell us what you're really after."

Another detective occupied the chair next to Ramos. Slight of frame and with short hair and a forgettable face, he hadn't said a word. Maddock had no doubt who the alpha dog was in this partnership. He jumped in before Bones said something to make their situation worse.

"Detective, I can appreciate what it looks like, but I want to make sure my girlfriend is safe. You didn't seem to be taking the situation seriously so we decided to look around and see what we could find."

"So we can add a charge of interferin' with a police investigation?"

"I'm sorry. You mean you were still conducting an investigation here? I noticed all the crime scene tape is already gone and the fingerprint dust cleaned up."

"You were messing around with my crime scene, Maddock. By definition, you're interferin'."

"Dude, you didn't even know the records storage room was part of the crime scene," Bones added.

Ramos' face went scarlet. "It doesn't matter."

Maddock sighed. "Fine, whatever. I told you why we were there. If you're not going to listen to us, then get us an attorney."

Ramos licked his lips and raised his eyebrows. "Why? You fellas got something to hide?"

Bones laughed. "Ramos, don't tell me that line actually works on anyone with a double-digit IQ."

Ramos showed the first signs of anything other than annoyance by displaying a set of crooked teeth. "Hey, it was worth a try. But seriously, once the lawyers are around, I can't do nothin' for you. Tell me this, why did you assault Sarah Abrams yesterday?"

Bones and Maddock shared a puzzled look. Maddock said, "Assault? What are you talking about?"

"You heard me. You expect me to believe there was a break-in and an assault one day and then you boys just happened to break in the next?"

Maddock shook his head. "This is pointless. Attorney. Now."

Ramos' hands caused the table to creak as he raised himself from his seat. "Have it your way. You may be here a while."

The door swung open and a woman entered. "No, Dwayne, they won't."

The woman had walked with a slight limp through the door, but aside from that she conveyed nothing but competence. Red hair that hung just below her shoulders, a trace of freckles, blue eyes with the slightest trace of green. She reminded Maddock of someone.

"I want to believe!" Bones exclaimed.

The newcomer rolled her eyes and Maddock realized that Bones had identified the resemblance to Special Agent Dana Scully from the show *The X-Files*.

She pointed at Bones. "Like I've never heard that before. You don't do too well with the ladies, do you?"

Bones' eyebrows wrinkled and he looked at Maddock. "The one on TV is much nicer. Smarter, too."

"If you two are done with your fantasizing, perhaps we could talk about why I'm actually here."

Ramos snorted. "Boys, this is Lieutenant Sandra Sterling. What a surprise. Yes, tell us why *are* you here? Last time I checked, this was just the lowly Mount Vernon District Police Station, not Club Fed over in McLean."

"Dwayne, my friend, I'm about to do you a big favor. I'm about to relieve you of responsibility for dealing with these lowlifes. No thanks are necessary. " She handed him a sheet of paper which he glanced at before folding it and stuffing it in his breast pocket.

"Us country bumpkins not quite up to your high-tone Park Police standards?"

"Lose the chip on your shoulder, Dwayne. It's unattractive, and you need all the help you can get in that department. We all know you were raised in the canebrake and pulled yourself up by your jockstrap to graduate from William and Mary. With two break-ins and an assault on National Park property, it was a question of when, not if, we got involved."

Ramos held her stare for several seconds. Then he shrugged and reached for the key to the cuffs which secured Maddock and Bones to the interview table. Maddock massaged his wrists as he stood, glad to be free of the confinement.

With a move so quick that Maddock barely saw it coming, Sterling slapped a cuff around one of his newly free wrists. "Not so fast, Mr. Maddock. The three of us are going to have a little talk somewhere more private. The cuffs mean that I won't have to worry."

Bones held out his arms, palms up. "I like a woman who accessorizes. And you don't have to worry about us, we'd never hurt you."

Sterling regarded him the same way Maddock recalled his second-grade teacher looking at a student who tried to eat chalk. "I'm not worried about that, Bonebrake. If one of you tried something and I had to take you down, it wouldn't look good on your service records. I don't want that on my conscience."

Bones turned to Maddock as, both cuffed, they followed her out of the room. "Any chance she's an alien, because I want her to probe me."

Maddock failed to suppress a chuckle and Sterling didn't turn as she replied over her shoulder. "Don't push me, Bonebrake. Be a shame to have to shoot you before you can answer any of my questions."

FOUR

"I'm telling you, man, she's actually with the CIA. Didn't you see the signs?"

Maddock tried to contain his irritation. Bones was annoying him, but his real beef was with the fact that he was locked in another interrogation room after nearly an hour trapped in the back of a Park Police vehicle. With the sun just coming up after a sleepless night, he was ready to lash out at whatever target presented itself. He wished he could take the sort of calming breaths that Melissa did to combat stress, but that sort of passive approach had never worked for him.

He exhaled anyway. "Bones, just because we drove past Langley doesn't mean that she's CIA. I know the Park Police has headquarters in the same area."

Bones shook his head sadly. "What better way to hide the affiliation than in plain sight?"

The door opened, and Lieutenant Sterling strode in. The door closed behind her of its own volition, as if scared that failure to do so would trigger Sterling's ire. Maddock actually didn't detect much anger in her, just intensity.

The room was nicer than the one in the Mount Vernon police station in that it had a window and at least looked like it had been painted during Maddock's lifetime. His hands were cuffed but not secured to the table, so that was something. But he was still trapped against his will. He heard the snarl in his own voice. "Lawyer. Now."

Sterling raised one eyebrow. "What makes you think you're entitled to one? You're not suspected of any crime."

"Fine," Maddock said. "In that case, you can take off these handcuffs and we'll be on our way."

She gestured with her index finger and shook her head. "A person of interest, that's what you are. We can hold you for at least twenty-four hours. I hear you SEALs can practically hold your breath for that long, so it should be a piece of cake to do it in an air-conditioned room like this one."

Bones said. "How about you just let Maddock go and you can interrogate me? There are all sorts of things I can tell you... and show you."

Sterling's smile was genuine, but more predatory than joyous. She yawned and stretched her arms above her head, and Maddock had to conjure an image of Melissa to keep his mind from focusing on how she moved.

Sterling stepped behind Bones and put her hands on his shoulders. Almost instantly, Bones' face tightened in an obvious attempt not to show any pain. Maddock even noticed traces of red creeping into the skin around his neck. "They call you Bones, right? A little predictable but it could be worse. Bones, I really don't think you want to be alone in a room with me."

A second later she released the pressure, and Bones let out a breath. She moved back around them and spoke to Maddock as if the previous seconds had never happened. "On the other hand, if you just answer a few questions, you'll be free to go in a matter of minutes. Well, unless you're interested in seeing some security footage of the break-in at Mount Vernon."

This time, Maddock looked at Bones before answering, but his friend looked equally confused.

"Okay. Lieutenant, you have our attention. Let's watch the video."

"Not so fast. A man has to take me to dinner before I invite him back to my place. First you answer some questions. Like what were you doing there last night?"

"Like I told Detective Ramos, we were worried about my girlfriend Melissa and her boss, and we wanted to see if we could find any clues."

"You thought you could do better than Dwayne Ramos?"

"I think my Mom could do better than that assclown," Bones interjected.

She considered that for just a second before barking a

laugh. "Fair point. Okay, did you find anything?"

The men shook their heads.

"And you're sure there was no other reason you were there besides trying to protect your girlfriend?"

Maddock nodded. "What other reason would there be?"

Sterling said, "No reason, apparently. I did a little research on your backgrounds. A bunch of it is classified, which seems strange for two guys not long out of SEAL training. But you seem to have been around the edges of a few civilian crimes recently as well. It's actually quite interesting."

Bones started nodding. "That's right, and there's more where that came from if you'd just--."

She didn't allow him to finish. "Bones, cancer cells are interesting too. Don't let it go to your head. I have another question for you. Have you ever heard of a group called the Sons of the Republic?"

Maddock knew he hadn't managed to keep the surprise from his face when he heard the words. He took a moment to gather his thoughts, but Bones had no such need.

"Hell yes, we've had a few run-ins with those jokers. They're big on 'taking the country back to its origins.' Maddock and I had to step in and bust a few of their heads when they got all upset at us disrupting their plans."

For the first time, Sterling looked at Bones with something other than ironic scorn. "What else can you tell me about them?"

Maddock was pretty sure Sterling already knew that he and Bones had encountered the Sons of the Republic before. If she had done her homework on them and knew about the Sons herself, she could have figured it out. In fact, her stepping in to rescue them from Detective Ramos made more sense in that context. He gave voice to the next logical thought.

"You think they're the ones who broke into Mount Vernon?"

"I can't say anything for certain, Maddock, but doesn't it seem to you like something they'd do?"

Maddock considered that. It was possible, but still a shot in the dark without evidence linking the group to the break-in. "Sure, but what reason do you have to think it was them?"

Sterling frowned, her aggressive manner all but gone. "Nothing I can put my finger on. But I've got a couple of sources who say they've been poking around in Virginia in recent months."

Bones asked, "What sources are those?"

Sterling grinned. "A woman never tells. Neither do the Park Police. At this point, I'm just trying to see the pattern and figure out motive."

Maddock shook his head. "I wish we could help you and I really do mean that. But unless they're trying to find some more concrete evidence that Washington…"

She arched an eyebrow. "Washington what?"

Maddock sighed. "You know what, forget I said anything. It's not going to help you figure out the break-in or find them."

"Plus if we told you, we'd have to kill you." Bones grinned.

Sterling looked from Maddock to Bones and back again. "I'll let that go. For now. In any case, I'll show you the video now if you're still interested."

Maddock nodded. She took out the key to the handcuffs and released both men. "Follow me."

The room with the stand containing the VCR and television was only a few steps down the hallway. It was really more of a closet than a room, a windowless space with weak lighting and a stack of chairs against one wall. Sterling fired up the A/V once Maddock and Bones had crammed themselves into the tiny chairs.

"It goes without saying that you two need to keep anything you see to yourself."

Maddock sensed that she expected a response, so he grunted an affirmative sound that seemed to satisfy her. The picture came on, a view of the storage room at Mount Vernon before Maddock had crashed half of the shelves.

On the screen, a man, Caucasian with short hair, moved hastily through the maze of shelves, checking the tag on every box. He was dressed in nondescript clothing—khakis, a polo-style shirt, and a jacket, zipped halfway up. Nothing that would stand out among the tourists at Mount Vernon. He had a drawstring bag slung over his shoulder. Maddock wondered if it held the fake Washington portrait.

"No sound on this?" Bones asked.

"Nope, just basic security footage."

They all continued to watch as the man searched the shelves. He finally found what he was looking for. He opened the box, rummaged through it, took out a paper inside a protective sleeve, and stuffed it inside his bag. He paused and cocked his head as if listening. He must have heard something because he hastily put the box back on the shelf, the wrong shelf, and hurried out. As he made his way back to the door, the camera caught the front of his face for a fraction of a second. It wasn't the sharpest image, but it was something.

Maddock asked. "Any luck on matching the face?"

Sterling said, "Not yet. We're trying to get some time on the FBI computer, but you can imagine how inter-agency cooperation goes sometimes. Do you recognize him?"

Maddock shook his head, not wanting his voice to betray his thoughts. Bones said, "You think that guy is one of the Sons?"

Sterling shrugged. "That's what I'm trying to find out. I hoped you might have seen him before."

Maddock detected a trace of deception in her eyes. "I have a question for you. Why are you so interested in this? I couldn't help notice that during our time here, you haven't written down a single thing or engaged one of your fellow officers. So please don't tell me it's just another case you've been assigned. "

Her blue eyes hardened. "I have my reasons."

"I'm sure you do. And if you want our help, I'd like to know what they are."

Sterling's eyes didn't change, but her lower lip puffed as

she exhaled with force. "You aren't wrong. My level of interest has little to do with my job. While I did officially take on your case last night, I don't expect it will remain assigned to me for long. There are some people who would rather this subject remained closed. That said, I don't intend to give up on unofficial pursuit of the Sons of The Republic. It's personal, and that's all I'm going to say right now."

Maddock looked at Bones, who appeared absorbed by their questioner. "Um, Bones. . ."

His head snapped back to see Maddock's inquisitive look. "Huh? Oh, yeah, that's good enough for me. Let me tell you about the last time we ran into the Sons..."

Maddock cut him off. "We can give you one name, Edmonia Jennings Wright. She's the majority shareholder in a Delaware company called the Vindication Corporation. As near as we can tell, the Sons have only a loose structure, but it's safe bet that she'll be involved in a lot of their activity."

"What was the last you heard of her?"

Bones chuckled. "That would be when she took you down with a flick of the wrist, right Maddock? The chick is like a hundred years old, but she's some kind of grandma ninja."

Sterling's face almost showed amusement, and Maddock had to focus to keep his cheeks from reddening. "Unfortunately, Bones is right, although she's more like seventy, not a hundred. I'm sure you can find her easily enough. Once it was clear she wasn't interested in coming after us, we stopped thinking about her."

Sterling's voice was flat. "Looks like you need to start again. I realize you don't know me at all, but trust me on this."

Maddock wanted to protest, but he thought about Melissa. If there was any chance Sterling was right about the involvement of the Sons, Melissa was probably in danger. Confronting Wright was the best option for solving that problem.

Second-best option, he corrected himself. There was another.

FIVE

"You know, Bones, You acted like a teenager with a crush on Lieutenant Sterling," Maddock said softly as they traversed the dark street. Up ahead, an old, gothic-style house loomed against a cloudy sky. It was their destination, and a foreboding one.

Bones frowned at Maddock. "Dude, you know me better than that. Don't I hit on pretty much every hot chick?"

"I don't think she's the sort you need to be messing with. She seems clever enough to get you to let your guard down."

Bones' brow crinkled. "Come on. Did I tell her anything that would compromise us?" Maddock opened his mouth, but Bones continued. "No, I didn't. Sandra Sterling is one hot babe and I was slipping her the old Bonebrake charm. You need to worry about yourself instead of micromanaging me."

Maddock wanted to argue, but he realized his friend was right. He knew the danger to Melissa was messing with his head and he wasn't reacting the way he normally did.

"Sorry, Bones, I guess you have a point. You think you could at least lay off the charm some? It can get awfully thick."

"I don't know, Maddock, that's asking a lot. Mostly it just comes naturally. I just ooze it."

"Like pus?"

Bones winced. "That's cold. Anyway, since we're sort of working for her now, I guess I'll try to rein it in." He paused. "I guess we're not exactly working *for* her. We just agreed to do a little investigating and let her know what we find out."

"We agreed because she's holding the threat of charges over our head like a Sword of Damocles."

Bones grimaced. "How about you quit trying to act smart and let's focus?"

Maddock and Bones stood in the shadows watching a gate set into a stone wall which surrounded a residence on the outskirts of Baltimore. After catching a few hours of daytime sleep and then making sure Sarah Abrams and Melissa were doing fine, he and Bones had driven north into Maryland. The house behind the fence belonged to Edmonia Jennings Wright.

He hadn't lied to Sterling when he said they knew about Wright but hadn't bothered to pursue her. However, he had committed a sin of omission by not telling her another key fact: he and Bones had recognized the face on the video from Mount Vernon.

The face belonged to a man he had last seen in a Philadelphia cemetery while recovering a lost document penned by Ben Franklin. At the time, the man had pointed a gun at Maddock while Edmonia Jennings Wright snatched the document for the Sons of the Republic. Maddock had thought that only Wright escaped during the ensuing firefight, but apparently so had this man.

When they had left the park police building early that morning, Maddock had figured finding the man would be their best route to getting more information on what the Sons were up to. But their normal source for information, a reporter named Jimmy Letson who had rung out of SEAL training, had apparently met a girl and was on a cruise in the Caribbean. They were on their own for a few more days at least.

Which meant taking a more direct route. Bones hadn't been far off in calling her grandma ninja, and as much as Maddock wanted payback for how she had taken him down so quickly, he knew better than to rush in without any planning.

"It's just surveillance for now, Bones, no breaking and entering. Figure out if she has any patterns we can exploit."

"You're no fun. Whatever happened to the man who said if a cop tried to stop us for speeding, we'd ignore him?"

"I can deal with a public servant. Edmonia Jennings Wright requires an entirely different level of caution."

Bones shifted his right shoulder, which leaned against one of several spruce trees combining with the darkness to give them cover. "For now, I'm with you. It sure seems weird that she doesn't have any lights on out here by the street. We could walk right up to the fence and no one would see us. Then again, this place looks like Edgar Allan Poe's ghost might hang out in the attic. Not sure I'm exactly dying to check it out."

Maddock handed their night vision goggles to his partner. They had acquired this pair on one of several recent classified missions, from an enemy who no longer numbered among the living.

"Look through here, Bones. Tell me what you see."

Bones took a long look. "Two cameras on the gate and a couple more on the wall itself. Looks like one of those combo infrared and regular jobs. Those things are not cheap."

"That tells me that Wright would rather not advertise her vigilance by lighting things up, but if anyone tried to breach she'd be all over them."

"How about we just follow that car that's pulling up to the gate?"

A vehicle with only basic running lights pulled up to the gate, which opened as if on command. The car wasn't anything special, just some sort of small sedan. The gate began to close before the car was even all the way through.

"Too late now, Bones. Prepare to do some waiting."

An hour went by, with nothing to do but take turns looking through the goggles. They speculated about what the Sons might be after, but neither of them really had any idea. The monotony was broken by the same car pulling back out through the gate. Maddock and Bones didn't even have to communicate the decision to set out for their rental car at a near run. They hopped in and pulled out from the curb before the sedan disappeared around the first corner in the street.

As they eased into a position a hundred feet behind the sedan, Bones asked, "How are we going to play it?"

"Seems like the best play is to follow him until he stops somewhere. A lot of things could go wrong if we try to take him in a place we're not familiar with while he's still in the car."

"I love a good carjacking, but you're right."

Maddock knew that following someone rarely turned out like it did the movies. Unless the person being followed had some reason to worry about surveillance or was trained to automatically check for it, following someone via car was easy. The ten-minute drive before their target pulled into a driveway next to a small house did nothing to prove otherwise.

Bones and Maddock stepped out of their rental as a man emerged from the car and walked up the steps of a porch illuminated by a single exterior floodlight. They were parked about fifty feet beyond the house, in a neighborhood with tiny houses and almost non-existent yards. Maddock gave silent thanks that the streetlight in front of the house the man had entered was burned out, allowing him and Bones to remain in the shadows as they approached.

He signaled with his hand for Bones to head around to the back through a narrow passage next to the driveway. Bones nodded, and Maddock made his way onto the porch, stepping carefully to minimize any creaking. He eased the doorknob to the left and was surprised when it turned without any resistance. Stopping his motion, he glanced through the pane of glass to the left of the door.

A white sheer drape did little to hide the fact that the door opened into a small entry room. He saw no sign of anyone in the room, so he took a breath and stepped through the door. He kept his eyes peeled in front of him as he slowly shut the door behind him.

The entry room had a single doorway other than the one through which he had come, and he moved toward it. The next room appeared to be some kind of living room with a faded brown couch. On the other side of that room was a doorway to a kitchen. He could see the back of a man with his left hand on an open refrigerator door, peering inside.

Maddock moved at an angle through the living room until he stood just to the left of the door to the kitchen. He took a second to go over in his mind how he would move into the kitchen and confront the target. Without further pause, he lunged into the kitchen.

To stare straight up the barrel of a huge pistol.

He was close enough to read the words *Israel Military Industries* on the side of the barrel. He recognized the Desert Eagle fifty caliber gun as a popular choice among enthusiasts who secretly doubted their own adequacy. He had to admit that it was doing the job right about now. The gun was so close that he began to move his arm and body into a close quarters anti-firearm defense move, but the man holding it had already started to slide backward as Maddock entered the room. Maddock arrested the movement once he realized that his window of opportunity had passed.

"Smart move. Hands in the air now." The voice was low and possibly even would have sounded pleasant had the circumstances been different. Maddock raised his hands.

"Who are you and what are you doing in my house?" Maddock could see the face now, and while he didn't recognize it, he did recognize the cold seriousness in the dark eyes.

"I was lost and I…"

The barrel dropped and a bullet tore through the unfinished wood an inch from Maddock's feet. "You think I'm a moron? Don't insult my intelligence. I saw you and your friend following me miles back. By now, he's discovered that there is no back door to this place and his only other option is to come through the front into the line of fire. So try again."

Maddock said the only thing he could think of. "Edmonia Jennings Wright."

The man flinched at the mention of the name. "What about her?"

"I need to speak with her."

He chuckled. "Make an appointment, like everyone

else."

Maddock shook his head. "I don't think that would end well."

"I got news for you. Breaking into my place is going to end even worse."

Maddock thought about saying that he hadn't broken in, but then a loud thump sounded from somewhere in the darkness. He saw the man's fingers tighten around the Desert Eagle's grip and his eyes darted from side to side.

That was all Maddock needed. He sprang forward and to the left, keeping his body outside the man's line of fire and to his 'gun side' to slow his reaction time. He'd studied more than his fair share of martial arts, including Krav Maga. Given the right set of circumstances he could disarm a person with a handgun, and a distracted man was best. He grabbed the barrel of the Desert Eagle with his left hand, pushing it away, and drove his right fist into the surprised man's chin. Before he could yank the pistol free, another fist flew out of the darkness, sending the man to the floor.

Bones stood there, grinning and rubbing his fist.

"What took you so long?"

"Just giving you a chance to handle it yourself. I know how you hate me making you look bad."

Maddock shook his head as the big man maneuvered their captive face-first onto the couch, held in the position by a knee in the upper back. Bones allowed the man's chin to extend just over the arm rest so that he could talk, which also meant that even relatively minor pressure exerted on the neck would result in excruciating pain.

The man remained defiant. "How the hell did you get in here?"

Bones said, "Through the bulkhead."

"But that was protected by a padlock I know you couldn't have cut through silently."

"Yeah, but you morons skimped on the chain."

Bones held up a rusted chain, with one of the links twisted out of position. A padlock connected two ends further down the chain. "Come to think of it, this is just what I need. You like necklaces?"

"What?"

"Or maybe they'd make good handcuffs."

Bones jerked the man's hands behind his back, eliciting a grunt of pain from his captive as he wrapped them around the man's wrists. He adjusted his knee, which now held both the chained hands and the man's upper back in place.

"What's your name? And don't take too long or I might get tired and have to rest my elbow on your neck."

The man's shoulders sagged and his eyes fell. "Dennis Guter."

Bones nodded to Maddock, who picked up the questioning. "Tell us why the Sons of the Republic broke into Mount Vernon."

Guter gaped, his eyes wide with surprise. He would have made a terrible poker player. When he spoke, even he didn't sound like he believed what he was saying. "Mount Vernon? I don't know what you're talking about."

Bones open-handed him on the ear. "Sure you do. You just think good old Edmonia is scarier than we are." He cracked his knuckles. "Let me know how badly we have to hurt you to change your mind and I'll get started."

Guter moved his neck half an inch to meet Maddock's eyes.

"Don't look at me," Maddock said. "He may be the bad cop, but there's no scenario where I'm the good cop."

Guter sighed. "You're killing my neck. Just let me up and I'll tell you. I promise I won't try anything."

"No can do. I know how much to trust a white man's promise. Tell us first and if you don't piss me off too much, maybe we'll let you up."

"Okay, okay. The Sons broke into Mount Vernon to find something that belonged to George Washington."

"And in other news, the sky is blue and disco sucks," Bones said.

Maddock shook his head. "Tell us something we don't know. It was Washington's home. Of course it has to do with him. What were the Sons looking for?"

"I don't think Jamison found exactly what Edmonia hoped for, but he did bring something back."

Maddock stopped him. "Who's Jamison?"

"The guy who broke into Mount Vernon. I thought you knew that."

Maddock said, "I knew his face but not his name. Go on."

"For some reason, Edmonia has been fascinated lately with Lafayette. She's been collecting his papers and correspondence. She found out that Washington promised to give Lafayette something big, something incredible."

"What would that be?" Maddock asked.

"I don't know, and if she knows, she's playing it close to the vest. Anyway, we found out a letter from Washington to Lafayette, one that was never mailed, had recently been discovered and sent to Mount Vernon. It told Lafayette where to look for something, a paper with some kind of clues on it. That's all I know."

"How did Wright know about the letter?"

Guter said, "She's Edmonia Jennings Wright. She's got access to stuff the NSA wishes it had."

"What did he find?"

"I don't know."

Bones exerted some additional pressure with his knee and Guter winced.

"Ow! Ow! I have no idea. I never even saw it! I just know he recovered something. Jamison is supposed to wait twenty-four hours in case he's being surveilled and then deliver it to Ms. Wright."

Bones raised his eyebrows and Maddock gave a slight nod. The big man let up the pressure a bit and said, "Which would be right about now, right?"

Guter nodded.

Maddock lowered his head so it was closer to the position of Guter's. "What's the endgame? What does Edmonia hope to ultimately find?"

"I can't say for certain. I just know it has something to do with Joan of Arc."

SIX

Cyrus Jamison maintained a healthy respect for the combat abilities of Edmonia Jennings Wright, despite the sheer improbability of a woman her age wielding such skill and maintaining such physical prowess. Whatever it was that kept her strong and fit, it bordered on magical. He feared no man or woman, but he practiced ruthless objectivity when it came to evaluating the skills of others. Wright's talent for martial arts placed her in a select and lethal group populated mostly by individuals serving in Special Forces from various nations and eastern practitioners who devoted their lives to it. Nearly all such individuals were male and between the ages of twenty and fifty.

Jamison still didn't know exactly how Wright had come by her skills. But he was quite sure that the planet contained no other woman over seventy who could best her. Hell, a lot of men many years her junior couldn't handle her. As her sometime sparring partner, Jamison knew that his equal skills and relative youth could defeat her, but only if he maintained the proper focus.

Consequently, his respect for her was genuine, not that of a subordinate trying to remain in his employer's good graces. Wright seemed to know this, as she didn't speak down to him the way she did nearly every other person with whom she came into contact. She had summoned him to the office at the Baltimore house for a late night discussion about the document he had retrieved the previous day.

Seated behind a large mahogany desk which amplified awareness of how slight her figure was, she wore the same baggy black pants and shirt as always. In her own home, she rarely wore the nylon top with the back hood that added an aura of mystery to her appearances in public. Her brown eyes promised a combination of secrecy and disappointment. The ornate sconce to the left of the desk gave off a soft light and left a lot of shadows in the room.

"I understand Dane Maddock appeared on the scene shortly after your departure. Will I never be rid of that man?"

It was a rhetorical question, so Jamison chose not to reply.

"I understand he now refers to me as Grandma Ninja."

Jamison chuckled. "It's not what they call you. It's what you answer to."

"Quoting Bill Clinton is beneath you, Cyrus." A sly grin creased her face. "I kind of like it myself. It conveys a certain respect while allowing those boys to retain some small fraction of their fragile egos. In any case, I believe you have something for me."

Jamison handed her a yellowed page inside a protective envelope. He had liberated it from Mount Vernon during the break-in, but as previously agreed he had waited twenty-four hours before making delivery.

"And the painting?" Wright arched an eyebrow.

"Switched out for the fake."

Wright nodded and then removed the sheet from the envelope. "This is in George Washington's hand. I recognize it. Unfortunately, it tells us nothing we don't already know."

"Not entirely," Jamison said.

Frowning, Wright cleared her throat and began to read.

"My Dear Marquis,

I regret that I must forego the warm greetings which I would normally extend to you. I have fallen gravely ill and fear these hours will be my last. You will recall I have previously made reference to a secret which I intended to share with you at the proper time. Should I expire before you again return to these shores, this letter and another item of great import I shall entrust to the most reliable man I know. I pray you may rest your head at Mount Vernon one last time. You guard *the secret.*

Yours affectionately,
G Washington"

Wright raised her head. "I assume the other item was

the journal, but what in this letter do you consider new information?"

"The last sentence. 'You guard the secret.' Present tense, with emphasis on 'guard' for some reason."

"So?"

"It occurred to me that the letter could be taken literally, so I went to the place where Lafayette would have rested his head."

"The Lafayette bedroom," Wright said.

Jamison nodded. "Facing the bed is…"

"A portrait of Lafayette," Wright finished.

"I found these hidden inside, affixed to the back of the painting." He reached inside his jacket and took out another envelope.

"You know how I feel about people who waste time on theatrics," Wright said. "Give me those."

Chastened, Jamison handed them over. "I can tell you they are pages from a personal journal, written in a cipher. I decoded them." He handed her a folded sheet of paper.

Wright looked it over. "This can't be all of it."

"Not even close. The person to whom Washington entrusted the journal must have only hidden the first two pages behind the painting and kept the remainder for himself. I hope what you're looking for hasn't already been found."

Wright closed her eyes and took a deep breath before opening them again. "I suppose it's possible, but I doubt it. Something like that would be difficult to keep hidden. I'm certain it never reached Lafayette. I've exhausted the possibilities on that score." She paused. "Now we need to figure out who, exactly, Washington considered the "most reliable man" he knew.

Outside the window, Maddock and Bones exchanged glances.

Sneaking onto the grounds of Wright's home had been child's play. Dressed in black and following Jamison's car through the gate had ensured they would remain undetected.

Eavesdropping on Wright and Jamison in the study was no challenge, either. Bones' legendary stealth and the fact that the desk was tucked into a bay window alcove allowed them to creep within a few feet of the woman and hear everything that was said.

They waited to hear more, but Wright dismissed Jamison. She took a long look at the translation her agent had given her, and then deposited it along with the letter in her desk. She rose to her feet and turned her gaze toward a large painting that dominated the far wall. Joan of Arc!

"My lady," she said, "I swear I will find it." With that, the woman sat down at the center of the floor, assumed a lotus position, and began to meditate.

"I think," Maddock whispered to Bones, "we should get busy."

SEVEN

Melissa was waiting when they arrived back at their motel room. Maddock hadn't wanted her to go home yet, just in case the Sons of the Republic wanted another go at the Mount Vernon staff. He wasn't worried about being discovered, as Bones had booked their room under the name Elvis Lennon, for reasons known only to him.

"I'm so glad you're all right!" she said as the two SEALs walked through the door. She threw her arms around Maddock, gave him a tight squeeze, and then quickly drew away. "What did you find out?"

"Right down to business, huh?" Maddock asked, a little disappointed she hadn't greeted him with a kiss.

"This is a scary situation and I want to know what's going on."

"Fill her in, Maddock." Bones dropped down on one of the queen beds, his size thirteen feet hanging off the end as they did nearly everywhere Maddock had seen him sleep.

Maddock quickly recounted what they had learned, omitting the part where a guy held a Desert Eagle in his face.

"It's obviously the mysterious journal they're looking for," she said. "That must be what Washington wanted Lafayette to have." She frowned. "But there's something I don't understand. Washington lived for several years after this letter was written, and he would have had opportunities to give the journal to Lafayette."

"Wright is certain it didn't get to Lafayette," Bones said quickly. He glanced at Maddock, who knew what his friend was thinking. *Avoid the subject of Washington's death.* Not for the first time, Maddock wondered if he'd always be forced to keep secrets from the people he cared about.

"Let's assume he went ahead and handed the journal off to this 'most reliable man.' Any idea who that would be?" Maddock asked.

A knock at the door cut off Melissa's reply.

Bones and Maddock sprang to their feet. Had the Sons found them?

"It's Sterling," a familiar voice said from the other side of the door.

"How did she find us?" Bones muttered as he headed for the door.

Sterling pushed the door open as soon as Bones had cracked it, forcing him to jump out of the way and back into the motel bathroom. She showed no signs of the brief detente from the previous day.

"You two haven't reported back to me," she said, closing the door behind her and locking it.

"We decided to stake out Edmonia Jennings Wright's house. We questioned one of her men, a guy named Guter, and he pointed us in the right direction."

Sterling crossed her arms. "And he just willingly shared the information with you?"

Bones stepped in front of her. "We can be very persuasive. Don't you want to hear what happened next?"

"I sure as hell don't want to hear what you did to get him to talk, but I doubt I'm going to like what happened next any better."

Maddock said, "No, you won't. You asked for our aid, so we took action. We got some information and we might need you to grease the rails as we move forward. So either head on back to Virginia or stop busting our chops and start working with us."

Sterling didn't back down, but some fire had left her voice. "You know I have the power to arrest you."

"Sure. But you already told us your pursuit is unofficial. My guess is that actually arresting us is the last thing you want to do."

She stared at Maddock for a long moment before lowering herself into a chair next to the room's small desk and lamp. "I'm not going to apologize, but I'll admit you have a point. Tell me what you know."

Maddock and Bones told her everything Guter had said,

as well as the subsequent events at Wright's house, including the presence of the man from the security video at Mount Vernon.

Sterling considered this. "So, any idea who Washington's trusted man was?"

"That's what we were talking about when you arrived," Maddock paused, a sudden thought hitting him. "You know what? I've been overthinking this!"

"No! Not you!" Bones jibed.

"Bite me. Anyway, I think I know who the person is."

EIGHT

The Smithsonian National Museum of American History stood on Constitution Avenue on the north side of the National Mall in Washington, DC. As they mounted the steps, Maddock stole a glance over his shoulder at the Washington Monument jutting up over the thin tree line. No matter how many times he visited the nation's capital, he found himself mesmerized by the history represented here.

"Not much to look at, is it?" Bones' sweeping gesture took in the museum's gray façade.

"It gets better on the inside. At least, it does if you like history."

"I hear they've got one of Elvis' outfits from his Vegas days in here."

"They've got a little bit of everything," Sterling said.

Maddock held the glass door for the others and the group proceeded inside. Five minutes later they were ushered into a tiny office with the name LISA ACIE etched on a nameplate beside the door.

Lisa Acie, a woman of medium height with light brown skin and long, lustrous black hair, greeted them with a warm, friendly smile and shook hands with each of them. Maddock didn't miss the way her gaze lingered on Bones as she invited them to sit.

"I have to say, I don't get many interview requests," she began, taking off her glasses and laying them on her desk. "What exactly can I help you with?"

"We're interested in Billy Lee," Maddock said. "We understand you're a descendant."

"That's correct." She was speaking to Maddock, but her eyes kept drifting to Bones. "His life is fairly well documented. I'm not sure how I can help you."

That was true. William "Billy" Lee was George Washington's slave and personal valet. One of the most trusted people in Washington's circle, he attended to

Washington's personal needs and filled a variety of roles. An expert horseman, he became Washington's huntsman, the man in charge of the hounds, on Washington's frequent hunting trips, and served him throughout the Revolutionary War and until his passing.

"The Smithsonian has a collection of Lee artifacts that are currently off display," Sterling interjected.

"That's true. It's a small collection. Is there something in particular you're interested in?"

"A journal," Maddock said.

"I'm sorry. If Lee kept a journal, it was lost over the years. There's no journal in the collection and no one in the family has mentioned one."

Maddock didn't miss the way her eyes flitted downward and her fingers twitched. She might not be lying, but something wasn't quite right.

"The journal we're looking for belonged to George Washington. We think he entrusted it to Billy on his deathbed, possibly to be passed along to Lafayette."

Acie froze, panic filling her eyes.

Bones reached out and took her hand. "Someone we care about is in danger because of this journal. If there's anything you can tell us…"

Acie's eyes moved to the open door of her office. "Close the door." When Bones had complied, she took a deep breath and closed her eyes. "I'm sorry. I don't know why I'm making such a big deal of this. It's just not something the family talks about."

Bones nodded. "Sort of like my great uncle's third…"

"Focus, Bones!" Maddock snapped.

Acie managed a grin. "You're right. Before he died, Washington entrusted a journal to Lee with instructions that it be passed along to Lafayette, but Lee only passed along a few pages and kept the rest for himself."

"Why?" Bones asked.

"Bitterness. Billy Lee was a trusted confidant, a friend to Washington. He stayed by Washington's side while this country fought a war in the name of freedom, yet he remained a slave until Washington's death. 'All men are created equal' my ass," she added under her breath.

"Makes sense," Bones said.

"Not entirely. Lee claimed that Washington broke his promise. He told his descendants that he actually remained enslaved for several years after Washington's death, but that doesn't make sense, since he was freed in Washington's will. The family just chalked it up to his alcoholism."

Maddock wished he could tell her that it did make sense, but now was not the time or place. Besides, Acie seemed to trust them. He didn't want to change that by revealing what would likely sound like a conspiracy theory.

"One historian said, *If Billy Lee had been a white man he would have had an honored place in American history because of his close proximity to George Washington during the most exciting periods of his career. But because he was a black servant, a humble slave, he has been virtually ignored.*" She shook her head. "Anyway, according to family tradition, the journal was written in code. Lee referred to it as his inheritance, and swore that one day he'd use it to give his family a better life. But, between his struggles with alcohol and the debilitating injuries he'd suffered in Washington's service, he declined fast and didn't leave Mount Vernon until he died."

"Did he pass the journal along to his descendants?" Maddock asked.

Acie nodded. "He did, but not until his death, almost thirty years after Washington died."

"What was in it?" Bones pressed. "What made it an 'inheritance'?"

"Again, all I know is the lore passed down through generations of our family. The journal was written in some kind of code, and by the time Lee's death approached, he was so far gone he claimed he couldn't remember why it had been so important. His descendants were poor and uneducated. Even if some of them wanted to decipher it, it's doubtful they would have been able to. And if they succeeded, what would they do with the information? Black freedmen held a station little above slaves."

"Could they have asked for help?" Maddock asked.

"Sure," Bones said. "Ask a white man for help. When has that ever gone wrong?"

Acie flashed a smile. "You know what I'm saying."

"Any idea what happened to the journal?" Bones asked.

Acie nodded. "Shortly after the end of the Civil War, one of my ancestors donated it to the Grand Army of the Republic."

"Never heard of it," Bones said.

"It was a fraternal organization of veterans of the Union army. They lobbied for causes related to patriotism and veterans' affairs. They even fought for voting rights for black veterans. My many-greats uncle was a veteran and admired the organization. He donated it with the condition that it be placed beneath the foundation of the memorial to Lincoln. That's all I know."

"Lincoln? Not Washington?" Sterling asked.

Acie shrugged. "Lincoln was the Great Emancipator. Washington set some slaves free, but not until he was dead and no longer had any use for them. Maybe that was it."

Sterling rose and offered her hand to shake. "Thank you for your help. We'll let you get back to your work."

"My pleasure." Acie handed a card to Bones. "Call me if I can be of further help."

"My schedule's tight just now, but I get back to DC from time to time." He gave her a wink, turned, and led the way out.

"I don't suppose your park service connections can get us access to the building records of the Lincoln Memorial?" Bones asked Sterling.

"I think they can. I'll take it from here. If I need you I'll get in touch." She pushed her way into the crowd of tourists and hurried away, her red hair marking her route."

"I guess that's it," Bones said. "This must be what chicks feel like when I make my early morning exits."

"Oh, this isn't it." Maddock turned to Bones and grinned. "I think Sterling's looking at the wrong monument."

NINE

"What do you mean Sterling's got the wrong memorial? There's only one Lincoln Memorial," Bones said.

"Want to bet on that?" Maddock enjoyed the confused look on his friend's face as they made their way out of the museum.

"All right," Bones said when they reached the sidewalk, "you've enjoyed your moment in the sun. Does this have something to do with all that useless history trivia you've got knocking around in that undersized head of yours?"

"It's hardly useless, at least, not right now."

"Get to the point, Maddock."

"The timing is all wrong. The Lincoln Memorial opened in the early 1920s. Now, it's possible that the Grand Army of the Republic held on to the journal for almost sixty years until the Lincoln Memorial was built, but I don't think so. I believe the journal was given for a specific monument that was in the works at the time. We'll have to check it out to be sure."

They rounded the museum, turned right on Constitution Avenue, and made the short walk to the District of Columbia Court of Appeals. There, gleaming in the sun, stood a white marble statue of Lincoln. The president, left hand resting on a fasces, a bundle of wooden rods, gazed out into the distance. It was a simple representation of the great man; not the massive, Olympian-like Lincoln that looked out onto the National Mall from the throne inside his famed memorial.

"It's not very big," Bones noted. That thing's not much taller than I am."

Indeed, the statue itself couldn't have been much more than seven feet tall, and the pedestal on which it rested not much taller than Maddock's almost six feet.

"It's big enough to hold a journal, but this pedestal worries me. It looks new."

They moved closer to the shiny granite base. LINCOLN was engraved on the front, while the back gave more information.

ABRAHAM LINCOLN
1809–1865
THIS STATUE WAS ERECTED BY THE CITIZENS OF
THE DISTRICT OF COLUMBIA APRIL 15 1868
RE-ERECTED APRIL 15 1923 UNDER ACT OF
CONGRESS OF JUNE 21 1922

"You're right, Maddock. 1868 would fit the timeline perfectly. And if Acie's ancestor, Lee's descendant, was gripped with Lincoln fever after the assassination that could explain why he wanted the journal put in a monument to Lincoln instead of Washington."

"True. He might even have seen it as forging a link between two great leaders. I'd imagine the Grand Army thought of it that way."

"But what about this last line? Re-erected? That's not good."

It was a measure of Bones' seriousness that he didn't make a bad pun out of the word. Maddock considered this. If the statue had been taken down and placed on a new pedestal, the journal might be lost. But he didn't want to give up so easily.

"Bones, can you create a diversion?"

"How big?"

"Don't get yourself arrested."

"Crap. I was ready to get naked." Bones looked around at the few pedestrians and grinned. "I'll come up with something." He moved out in front of the statue, cleared his throat, and boomed, "Who will emancipate the red man?"

Maddock grinned and hurried away. Bones was frequently full of crap, but he could get serious about the plight of Native Americans when he wanted to. As his friend launched into his impromptu speech, Maddock headed back to the sidewalk and found the nearest manhole. Traffic was light and the pedestrians were all looking up at Bones, so he slipped his fingers through the holes of the manhole cover and lifted the heavy circle, climbed in, and slipped it back into place. The fetid odor of stagnant water and decay assaulted his nostrils as he climbed down into the darkness. When he hit the bottom, he turned on his MagLite and moved through the low tunnel, heading in the direction of the statue.

He soon hit paydirt. In one section, the circular tunnel gave way to a square room constructed of crumbling bricks. Up above, he could just make out the muffled sound of Bones pontificating. Smiling, he shone his light up and down the cracked walls.

"*Beneath* the foundation," he said to himself. In one corner, he noticed a brick that was double the size of all the others. His heart began to race as he drew his Recon knife and chipped away at the mortar. It crumbled like sand beneath the sharp metal until, finally, the brick came free. He let out a small whoop of triumph and shone his light into the space where the brick had been.

Nothing.

"You've got to be kidding me." He reached in and felt around the empty space, but there was nothing there, save a bit of dust and one desiccated spider. Muttering a few choice obscenities, he hefted the brick and made to replace it when something thudded to the floor.

He froze and turned his light downward. The beam fell on a dried out oilcloth bag.

"It's a hollow brick, genius," he chided himself. Hope rising anew, he replaced the brick and then carefully opened the bag and peered inside.

The bag held a small, cracked, leather bound journal. He closed the bag, tucked it inside his shirt, and headed back the way he had come.

When he climbed back up to the manhole he paused to listen, but heard nothing. He doubted he would be able to hear approaching footsteps anyway. He raised the manhole cover an inch and peered out.

The few pedestrians were still looking toward the statue, but Bones was no longer making a speech.

As Maddock's eyes fell on his friend, Bones drove his fist into the chin of a thickset man, sending the attacker to the ground on rubbery legs. A second man stepped back and raised a pistol. Before Maddock could call out a warning, Bones lashed out with his foot, kicked the gun to the side, and bore the man to the ground. He slammed his attacker's head into the pavement and sprang to his feet.

"Bones! This way!" Maddock shouted.

Bones spotted him and took off at a dead run. Behind him, the first man he'd taken down had pushed himself up to a sitting position and looked with bleary eyes at Bones' retreating form.

"Why not just run away?" Bones gasped as he reached the manhole.

"In case there are more of them. Come on!"

Maddock dropped to the ground and then moved out of his friend's way. Bones landed heavily on his feet and they took off at a trot.

"Holy crap, these ceilings are low," Bones growled.

"I don't know if you can call the top of a sewer drain a 'ceiling', but whatever," Maddock said.

"Did you find anything?"

"Not much. Just Washington's journal."

"Did I ever tell you you're awesome? Well, no because it's not true, but you do find more nuts than the average blind squirrel."

Maddock laughed. "Thanks, Bones."

They passed through the chamber where Maddock had found the journal and then back into another low passageway. Maddock kept his eyes open for a way out, but saw nothing. After a few minutes, he held up a hand and they stopped.

"Do you think anyone's following us?" Bones whispered.

"That's what I'm wondering." He strained to listen, and finally heard the sound of footsteps moving in the distance.

"No idea how far away they are, but they're definitely after us."

"I should have grabbed that dude's gun."

"It's better if we get out of this with no killing. Come on."

They set off again, trying to move silently. Maddock could move almost silently, but next to Bones, his every movement sounded like thunder to his ears. Finally, they came to a cross-tunnel.

"Which way?" Bones asked.

Maddock chose a direction at random and hurried along. Behind them, the faint sounds of pursuit continued unabated. He picked up the pace, grimacing as they splashed through chill puddles of mud and stagnant water and slipped on detritus.

"Running hunched over like this is bad for my back," Bones grumbled.

"I could make a joke about you being accustomed to bending over, but that would be too easy," Maddock jibed.

"Screw you, Maddock."

A few minutes later Maddock came to a sudden halt.

"What is it?" Bones had the good sense to keep his voice down.

"Look over here." Maddock shone his light into a wide fracture in the side of the passageway. "There's something back there. An old cellar, maybe. Think you can squeeze your giant butt through?"

"If that swollen head of yours will fit, I should have no problem." Bones slipped out of his leather jacket, took a deep breath, forced the air out of his lungs in a whoosh, and squeezed sideways into the narrow passageway.

Maddock watched his friend fade slowly into the darkness. The footsteps were coming closer. "Are you almost there?"

Bones let out a grunt and, with a dull scraping sound, forced his bulk out of the crevice. "Come on."

Maddock followed quickly, though his muscular frame made things difficult for him, too. When both were on the other side, they shone their lights around, looking for a way out.

They were in some sort of old cellar, forgotten by the looks of it. Dust and cobwebs coated the ancient brick walls, and black mold clung to the beams above their head.

"We need to find a way out, and quick," Maddock said. "If the Sons catch up with us, and we're waving these flashlights around, our side passage here is useless."

Bones quickly spotted a trapdoor in the ceiling at the far corner of the room. "There's no way up." He shone his beam down on a crumbling pile of wood that might have once been stairs.

"We'll have to do this in proper military fashion," Maddock said.

Bones grinned. "Just like the obstacle course. Let's do it."

They quickly positioned themselves beneath the trapdoor. Bones knelt and Maddock climbed onto his friend's shoulders. Maddock wasn't exactly a lightweight, but Bones had no trouble lifting the smaller man up.

Maddock tried the trapdoor. It wouldn't budge.

"Guess you'll have to bust through it." Bones' voice didn't indicate the slightest bit of strain at holding Maddock's solid one hundred eighty pounds. The man was a beast.

"Unless there's something heavy sitting on top of it."

"Always the optimist," Bones said. "Just try it."

Maddock drew back his hand, palm open. If this didn't work, the sound was certain to draw their pursuers directly to them. That could get ugly. Nothing he could do about it now. He threw all of his strength into the blow. He struck the soft wood with the heel of his palm, letting out a guttural *keop*, martial arts style. The trapdoor shattered like a movie prop. Two more blows and the way was open.

"Nothing like dry rot to make you look like a badass," Bones said.

Maddock climbed up into a pitch black room, turned and reached back to help Bones up.

"Don't bother. I got this." Bones took a few steps back and ran toward the corner below the trapdoor. He leaped up, kicked off of one side of the wall, and then the other, each push propelling him upward. With a grunt of effort, he caught the lip of the trapdoor with the tips of his fingers. "Okay. Help?" he gasped.

Under a different set of circumstances, Maddock would have let him fall as a punishment for his hubris, but they didn't have time. He grabbed Bones by the wrists and hauled his friend up.

"You're strong for such a little guy," Bones stood and reached out to tousle Maddock's hair, but Maddock knocked his hand aside. "So touchy. Where do you think we are?"

"A storage area." The beam of Maddock's light fell on crates marked COSTUMES and a heap of outdated lighting fixtures. "A theater, by the looks of it."

"Any prop weapons we can use? A spear or something?"

"Not that I can see, but let's try and make it tough on these guys." He hefted one of the crates and placed it over the gaping hole in the floor, and then leaned a few of the lighting fixtures onto it to add some weight. It wasn't much, but it might slow the Sons down. Now to find an exit.

Bones had already found the door. "Locked," he said after trying the knob. "But not for long." He lashed out with a powerful side kick and the door swung open with a sharp crack of breaking wood as the facing shattered.

Maddock shook his head. "You have the delicate touch of the finest craftsman."

"I get crap done. That's what matters."

They came out in a dark hallway that led to a narrow stairway. The dust beneath their feet bore mute witness to this being yet another forgotten, or at least lightly traveled, space. Faint, yellow light gleamed through the crack beneath the door at the top of the stairs, giving them hope.

"Wonder what we'll find on the other side," Bones mused.

"Can't be worse than what's behind us." Maddock

pocketed his MagLite and opened the door. As light poured in, a loud voice called out.

"Take one more step and you're dead!"

Maddock froze. Had the Sons of the Republic somehow gotten ahead of them? And then another voice rang out in the narrow hallway beyond the door.

"You don't understand. Just listen to me."

"What the hell have we stumbled into?" Bones asked.

"I don't know." Maddock listened. "They're somewhere that way." He pointed to his left.

"I'm through listening to you, Ryan," the first voice said.

"Justin, put the gun down!"

The sharp report of a pistol reverberated down the hall.

"I say we go the other direction," Bones said. He shouldered past Maddock and took off at a trot. They ascended another staircase and found themselves at another locked door. Bones didn't have to kick this one in. A little fiddling with the doorknob plus a bit of main force was all it took. He stepped through and stopped.

"It's a play."

"What?" Maddock moved to his friend's side and froze.

They stood on a small balcony overlooking a packed theater. To their left, two tiers, one for seating and one for lighting, looked down on the stage. The walls were painted cream and white, the carpet a bright red. Down below, heads turned their way as patrons noticed their presence. Someone pointed up at them and said something Maddock couldn't quite hear. An angry murmur rippled through the audience.

"This box is fancy," Bones said. "I wonder why no one's sitting here. The tickets must be too expensive."

For the first time, Maddock looked at the box in which they stood. American flags framed the small space, and bunting adorned the rail. His eyes fell on the antique chairs and his stomach lurched.

"Bones, this is Ford's Theatre." He swallowed hard. "And we're standing in the box where Lincoln was shot."

Bones' eyes went wide. "Holy crap. Let's get out of here."

Down below, Maddock saw two uniformed, armed security guards, scurry out of the theater. "I don't think we have much time."

Bones opened the door, looked out, and closed it again.

"Sons of the Republic coming up the stairs."

"That was quick," Maddock grumbled.

"I guess we'll jump."

"The last guy who tried that broke his leg," Maddock said.

"Was he a SEAL?"

"It was John Wilkes Booth."

"Three names? Sounds like a wuss to me." Bones turned and approached the rail. The actors on stage, probably distracted by the noise of the crowd, had stopped the play, and now stared up at Bones and Maddock in shock.

Bones didn't miss a beat. "You shot my brother!" he shouted at the actor who still clutched his prop pistol. "I'll kill you for that." He flashed a grin at Maddock and then vaulted the rail. He hit the stage with a loud thud, but regained his feet in an instant. As he rose to his full height, the actors on stage took one look at the massive Cherokee, turned, and ran.

Grinning, Maddock vaulted the rail, felt the tingling sensation of falling, and hit the stage. He felt the impact all the way up to the top of his skull, but he didn't think anything was broken. He stood and turned to the audience.

"There will be brief intermission and then our play will resume."

He and Bones leaped off the stage and sprinted up the aisle toward the exit. More shouts filled the air, this time from the direction of Lincoln's box. He stole a glance back and saw their pursuers, pistols in hand, turning to face the security guards who had just burst into the box.

"It'll be cool," Bones said. "The rent-a-cops will back down when they see those guys mean business."

"I hope so."

They dashed out through the tiny lobby and burst onto

the sunlit street. Navigating the throng of tourists, they ran aimlessly down the street, taking turns at random, until they finally managed to hail a cab.

"Where to?" the driver asked.

Maddock's thoughts drifted to the book. They'd need to find a way to translate it, but he wanted to get out of DC.

"Take us to the best bookstore in Alexandria, and I'll pay you double if you get us there in twenty minutes or less.

The cabbie accepted the challenge at once, put the pedal to the floor and screeched out into traffic to the tune of blaring horns.

"What's our next move?" Bones asked.

"Let's call Sterling," Maddock said. "We can't seem to shake the Sons, so we'll need all the help we can get."

TEN

Cyrus Jamison couldn't help but grind his teeth. He despised failure, and having to deal with Wright made it that much worse. Between her, Maddock, and Bonebrake, he wasn't sure whether to be more concerned about his enemies or his ally.

The loss of the journal was unfortunate, but that didn't trouble him. They would have it soon, thanks to Wright. The crafty woman seemed to know their every move before it happened, which was how he'd managed to put men on their tail yesterday.

After Maddock and Bonebrake had escaped, he'd wasted time cleaning up the mess at Ford's Theatre. Thankfully, his men hadn't shot anyone, and he had sufficient connections within the DC police to make the whole thing go away.

He debated his next move. Even if Maddock and Bonebrake remained in DC, it was a big city and he and his men couldn't catch them without Wright's help. Time was of the essence. The two SEALs were onto something; that much he could tell. After a few minutes of internal debate during which he had to force himself not to grievously injure one of his men who kept asking what they would do next, he accepted that he would have to report back to Wright, and he should do it in person.

The journey back was uneventful. A sense of deja vu hit Jamison as he once again entered Wright's house at an hour when most normal people were tucked soundly under the covers. He chuckled when he imagined what a nosy neighbor might think of the nocturnal activity. His focus sharpened upon entering the office.

"Sit, Cyrus."

With minor trepidation, he lowered himself into a padded chair.

Wright fixed him with a cool stare. "I've been waiting

for your report."

He stilled himself to calm. "We located Maddock and Bonebrake, and followed them to a very interesting location."

"Ford's Theatre."

Jamison paused. "I won't even ask how you know that. That's where we lost them, but it's not the first place they went." He went on to explain the details of what had happened, concluding with, "We didn't actually see it, but we're certain Maddock found the journal."

Wright gazed up at the portrait of Joan of Arc that hung from her office wall and nodded thoughtfully. "You are correct."

He couldn't hide his surprise. "What?"

"They did, in fact, find the journal. They have translated only a portion of it, but they learned enough that they have already left Washington DC."

"The journal, does it confirm that Washington had..." He didn't need to finish the thought.

Wright shrugged. "They haven't gotten far enough into the translation to know. We do, however, know whose treasure Washington sought." She paused. The few pages Jamison had recovered from Mount Vernon referenced a conversation a young Washington had with a dying man, but were maddeningly vague. "I also know where they are headed next."

A spark of resentment kindled in Jamison's chest, but it was quickly doused as relief flood through him. So it wasn't over.

"I'll give you the location." Wright's eyes suddenly locked with his, boring into him. "I must warn you, Cyrus. My patience grows thin."

"So, when he was young, George Washington ran into an old sailor who gave him clues about the location of Blackbeard's treasure, and this journal is the record of Washington's search for it? Sweet! Where do we look first?" Bones asked.

"I'm still a little surprised you don't already know where it is, with all your interest in strange myths." Maddock had lost count of the number of conspiracies and tall tales Bones accepted as gospel. Or at least claimed to accept; sometimes Maddock thought the big guy was just having fun with the crazy theories.

"Nah, I like things that make more sense, like the aliens at Roswell or the fact that Jimi Hendrix is alive and living in Hawaii with Jim Morrison."

Maddock had found a few helpful books on ciphers and set to work translating Washington's journal. Several times he nearly pinched himself, so amazed was he to possess such a treasure of American history. Though the first few pages were missing, he quickly realized that Washington was looking for treasure. As soon as the name Edward Teach, better known as Blackbeard, showed up, he had called Sterling and they'd set out for North Carolina. Sterling rode in the back, continuing the translation while Bones sat in the passenger seat, making everyone miserable.

Bones shook his head. "You know, I can't believe you brought me back to freaking North Carolina. You know how hard I worked to get out of this place."

"What's wrong with North Carolina?" Sterling's tone indicated that her patience with Bones was nearly exhausted.

"Rednecks. Lots of rednecks."

"Maybe not here, so much," Maddock offered. "It's more touristy here. Not like the part of the state where you're from."

They were at the Gull Rock Game Land Preserve near Engelhard, a tiny town on the outer banks of North Carolina. Just off the coast in Pimlico Bay, Blackbeard had gone down for the last time. It seemed a logical place to start.

"I hope not. You know how John Deere hats and NASCAR bumper stickers get on my last nerve. I'd hate to get arrested for battery or destruction of property."

"Speaking of last nerves," Sterling began, "I read a dossier on you, Bonebrake. It was short on personal details, but it did mention arrests; mostly when you've been drinking. I don't know if you really believe all this crap you spout, or if you're covering up something, but it gets old and it's distracting. If we're up against the Sons of the Republic, we're gonna need to be paying attention to as much as we can, so maybe cut the crap."

Bones looked surprised but recovered immediately. "The rumors of my drinking have been exaggerated." A smile crept across his face. "I'm growing on you, aren't I?"

Sterling couldn't keep a straight face. "Like a fungus. Okay, gentlemen, where to now?"

"The journal mentions Teach's Light. Supposedly on most nights you can see a weird light dancing over the bay out there." Maddock nodded toward the southeast, the direction from which a light breeze carried the smell of salt water. Darkness had already descended.

"Teach's Light?" Bones asked.

"The locals say that it's Blackbeard's ghost dancing. He went down out there in a battle with two British sloops. To make sure he was dead, the British commander, Lieutenant Maynard, cut off his head and hung it from the bowsprit. The legend says that the hanging head yelled '*Come on, Edward*' and then the beheaded corpse swum thrice around the boat before sinking."

Bones chuckled. "Now that's a bad dude. Either that or he's part chicken. Anyway, I'm always down for a ghost hunt."

Sterling said, "Let's not tell anyone we're out here looking for ghosts. Might draw the wrong kind of attention."

Maddock corrected her. "We're not looking for ghosts. We're just following clues. Washington underlined the words three times. He clearly thought it was significant, perhaps a signpost on the trail to the treasure. I figure it's worth checking out, unless we find something more in the journal."

"Not so far," Sterling said. "Notes from conversations he had with storytellers, mostly. He was trying hard to find this so-called light."

"If anyone can find it," Bones said, "Maddock and I can."

As evening fell, they set out, hiking various trails in the area where, legend had it, the light had been seen. Despite no sign of other human beings, the night was far from silent. Early on, they heard the occasional quack from the massive local duck population, and a constant the whole time was the buzzing and chirping of various insects. A few times they heard larger creatures moving through the swampy underbrush.

Checking a compass periodically, they tried to keep themselves close to the bay. They obtained many views of it via flashlight, but not once did they see anything which they could characterize as unusual lights, let alone actual ghosts. During a break around two in the morning, Maddock noticed Bones' unusual silence.

"Something on your mind, Bones?"

Bones didn't quite smile. "Nothing I can put my finger on, but I get the feeling we're not out here alone."

Bones expressing this kind of concern was rare enough that Maddock decided to give it a lot of weight. The man generally had good instincts.

"Any suggestions beyond just being extra vigilant?"

"Nah, not much we can do besides that. We're more likely to be attacked by boredom. What're we gonna do if Eddie Teach's ghost doesn't show himself by morning?"

"I have one idea, but it's a long shot and involves a lot of work. Let's just see out the night first."

"Okay, but I'm getting a little sick of this sleeping all day and staying up all night crap. Night time is party time."

Sterling and Maddock both laughed. They started moving again, and a minute later another one of the larger creature sounds erupted close to them. Maddock shined the flashlight in the direction of the sound, and for a few seconds he saw nothing.

A sudden sound, a rustling in the underbrush and the

thrum of feet broke the silence, and a herd of wild pigs burst from the bushes coming straight at them. The largest ones reached over three feet in height and a few of them had sharp tusks which reflected off their flashlight beams.

Almost as if they had communicated telepathically, Maddock, Bones, and Sterling turned and ran back the way they had come.

"That's a lot of bacon!" Bones shouted.

The stampeding pigs were now less than ten feet behind Maddock, who was bringing up the rear.

Maddock doubted they could outrun the animals, but he saw no other options. The tangled undergrowth on either side of the trail would slow them down too much. Even if he drew his Recon knife and turned to fight, what was the best he could hope for? Could he even kill one before he was run down by the herd?

Shots rang out from the darkness up ahead, interrupting his thoughts. He had only a moment to realize the herd had turned aside before something ensnared his ankles and he fell hard on his face. Before he could regain his feet, a huge weight fell on his back. Then he felt something grab and bind his hands. He reacted with a violent ripple through his body, beginning at his core and culminating with his legs chopping in search of a target while his face remained planted. The weight flew off his torso, but unfortunately his attack found only air. As soon as his legs struck the ground, someone grabbed and bound them.

He stopped resisting and rolled to his side. His flashlight lay a few feet away and in its beam he could make out Sterling similarly bound. He caught a glimpse of Bones thrashing on the ground, and called out.

"Come on, Bones, keep fighting."

A foot impacted his face and stars flashed across his vision. He sensed a shadow moving through the light beam toward where Bones lay, but he had to close his eyes and shake his head several times before he could see clearly again. When he could, he saw two men standing over a securely bound Bones. One of the men looked familiar, even

in the minimal light.
    Cyrus Jamison.

ELEVEN

The tight straps dug into Maddock's wrists and ankles, and rough pine bark itched his back where the tail of his shirt had ridden up. Sterling, similarly trussed, sat facing him, her face expressionless. He cast a sidelong glance at Bones, who leaned against a tree about ten feet away. The big Cherokee glowered at their captors.

"I can't freaking believe we let these idiots catch us. It's like the varsity just lost to the chess club."

Jamison stepped toward Bones, and his measured tone sounded more threatening than loud shouts could have. "Bonebrake, do you want a gag added to your restraints? We can arrange that."

Maddock thought Bones looked genuinely offended. He said. "Forget the gag, Jamison. What do you and Wright want?"

"We'll take the journal, for starters."

Sterling piped in. "What journal?"

"I was wondering when we'd hear from you, Lieutenant Sterling. I just didn't think you'd insult my intelligence by playing dumb."

Bones chuckled. "She's just trying to speak your language. If she used long sentences, we'd never be able to communicate with you." He shook his head. "Come on, do you honestly think we brought it with us? We're just bird-watching. Did you know the scientific name for a lot of ducks begins with *anas?*"

Jamison's face tightened for a moment. "We turned your vehicle inside-out and found the books on codes and ciphers. We know you have the journal. Where is it?"

"It's gone. I read it and then destroyed it," Maddock said.

"So I can kill these two?" Jamison inclined his head toward Bones and Sterling.

Maddock wanted to kick himself. He seldom spoke

without thinking things through, and this was an example of why.

"If you want my cooperation, you'll keep your hands off of all three of us."

Jamison cracked a sliver of a smile. "We could extract the information from you, but I figure you can stand up to interrogation, and I'm in a hurry. Tell you what. I'll keep you all alive. How long can you watch me cut pieces off of your best buddy before you give in?"

"Start with my junk," Bones said. "I can afford to lose several inches there."

Jamison's smile spread. "Let's see how much of that bravado is real. Where are the knives we took off of these two?"

Sterling broke immediately. "I have it." Her face turned beet red as all heads turned toward her. "But it's hidden, and you'll never find it."

Jamison stepped closer to her. "I'm not certain that's true, Lieutenant. I doubt you care about your two companions here, but I'll bet you have someone you wouldn't want any harm to come to No one is safe from the Sons."

Sterling's face going pale was visible even in the scattered flashlight beams. Her eyes targeted Jamison until he finally looked away. Then she spoke again. "Do what you need to do, Jamison. We've got all night."

Jamison turned to his men. "Did you frisk these three?"

"Frisk?" one man replied.

Jamison rolled his eyes. "If the book's not in the car, then one of them has it on their person."

In unison, the men cast nervous glances from Bones to Maddock, then back to Bones, before moving toward Sterling.

"Don't touch me you perverts!" She struggled as Jamison hauled her roughly to her feet. He waved his men away and gave her a brisk pat-down. He froze as his hand reached the small of her back, a triumphant smile creeping across his face. A moment later he held the journal in his hands. "That's settled, then."

Maddock tensed. What would Jamison do to them now that he had the journal, and was there anything he could do about it?

Jamison nodded at one of his men, who started jogging down the double-track dirt trail into the darkness. Then he allowed his eyes to roam across the three captives. "As much as I'd like to go ahead and kill you, Ms. Wright wants to speak to you before I do too much damage. We'll be going for a ride very shortly. For now, on your feet."

He reached for Sterling and pulled her up. She wobbled a bit, but managed to stay standing despite the bonds around her lower legs. Jamison did the same thing to Maddock, who launched himself forward at Jamison as soon as he was on his feet. Jamison easily moved out of the way, allowing him to crash face first into the ground. Maddock spit out some pieces of gravel and felt warm, sticky blood flowing across his nose as he shifted onto his side.

"Shall we try that again, Maddock? If you do the same thing, I assure you the result will be the same."

He hauled Maddock back to his feet. One of his men picked up Sterling and flung her over his shoulder like a sack of potatoes. She thrashed wildly about, but a sharp blow to the kidney caused her movement to subside. Maddock and Bones were too heavy to carry in a similar fashion, but moments later, a low rumble and the flash of headlights announced the arrival of one of Jamison's minions driving a four-wheeler. The men shoved Maddock and Bones into the back and hauled them away.

The journey ended at a faded white Mercedes Sprinter van. The back was already open and a ramp extended from it to the ground. Jamison had come prepared. What Maddock still couldn't figure out was how they had been found. Surely he'd have noticed if they'd been followed along the way.

The cargo straps loosened and two pairs of hands grabbed his limbs and lifted him with a jerk. He braced himself, expecting to be tossed into the back of the Sprinter.

What actually happened was worse. They folded him in half with his bound shins touching his head, and wrapped another restraint under his arms and around his ankles in a figure-eight. As they carried him up the ramp, he had no chance to generate any power. They secured him against the wall of the van with two tight straps which seemed designed to hold appliances.

A minute later, Sterling and Bones were secured against the opposite wall in a similar manner, although she remained in a seated position unlike Maddock. The only positive he could take was that his position allowed him to see his companions. He couldn't picture how they would escape, but he knew he needed to plan as if it would happen and maybe an opportunity would present itself. After the men had driven the four-wheeler up the ramp, parked it inside, and departed, he spoke to them in a whisper.

"Can you get loose?"

Sterling moved her wrists and ankles, looking for weaknesses. "Not my feet for sure. My wrists have a little play, but I'm not sure what I can do with them behind my back. I'm guessing you two are out of luck."

"You could say that. We got out of a lot of tight spots in SEAL training, but never bound quite like this.

Jamison and one of his men stowed the ramp and the closed the back door of the Sprinter. With no glass between the cargo area and the front, Maddock, Bones and Sterling found themselves in near-complete darkness.

Then the door opened again and one of Jamison's other two men jumped up into the back. The scowl on his face and the tension in his shoulders told the story of what he thought about having to ride in the back with them. Maddock had to hand it to Jamison, though. Leaving them back here unsupervised carried too much of a risk of them getting loose, no matter how well they were secured.

A gun appeared in the man's hand, some sort of automatic pistol from what Maddock could see.

"Listen you three, I ain't allowed to kill you. But nobody said anything about roughing you up. Anyone tries anything, they get a bullet in the leg. Are we clear?"

Almost as if by agreement, none of them responded verbally, but they all nodded. Apparently satisfied, the man tucked the gun into the waistband of his jeans and closed the back doors. Then he flicked on a flashlight, walked to the front wall which separated them from the cab, and lowered himself to the floor. From this position, he could easily see all three of the captives.

"What's your name?" Sterling asked.

"Steve. But it'd be best if y'all don't do much talking." With that, he placed the flashlight on his lap, angled so that it cast enough light for him to keep an eye on all of them.

The van started moving, slowly at first, bumping over what Maddock knew was the dirt road on which they had entered. Soon the ride smoothed out as they reached the paved road. Maddock turned his head toward Bones, wondering if he should risk conversation. Bones beat him to it.

"Yo, Steve, I gotta ask. Was your mama as ugly as you or did that come from the other side of your family?"

Steve's face tightened and his hand went to his gun. Maddock knew what Bones was doing; heck, Steve probably knew what Bones was doing, too. It was a dangerous game, but Maddock knew with certainty Bones would continue.

"No answer, huh? Well maybe you never knew your father, so you don't know the answer. Still, if I looked like you I think I'd make it my business to find out."

Steve got to his feet and pulled out his gun. Despite the rumbling of the wheels beneath them, Maddock detected no wavering in the man's hand. "You're a beat away from having an extra hole in you."

Bones met his eye with a glare that seemed almost comical given how trussed the big man was. "You're telling me you'd shoot a guy tied up like this just for making a couple of comments? Man, you must really be scared of me."

To better view the action, Maddock twisted his head to the side as much as possible. Steve took a step closer and then knelt so his head was down near Bones' head. "Scared of a man who got caught by a stampede of pigs? I don't think so. But I'd still have no problem shooting--."

With a lightning movement, Bones struck Steve's forehead with his own. Both the gun and Steve dropped to the floor. Maddock could recall when they had learned this move in SEAL training, the ability to headbutt someone with little or no momentum from three inches away. It required tremendous neck strength, and Bones had seemed a natural.

Bones blinked a few times and then grinned. "Like taking candy from a baby. A baby with a really hard head."

Maddock smiled back. "That was awesome. For your next trick you get loose, right?"

"Sorry, man. No way these are coming off. But at least we don't have to watch that guy sulk for hours."

"He's gonna wake up at some point, though. Or they're gonna stop and check on us."

Sterling said, "We may not have to worry about that."

They both turned to her. She held up one hand, which she had managed to free. "I pulled the old "angle the wrists" trick when they tied me up. They were so concerned with subduing you two bad-ass sailors that they didn't pay enough attention with me."

Maddock said, "When were you gonna tell us?"

She chuckled. "I was waiting for the right time."

"I told you she was worth hanging around with, Maddock. Free me next, Sandra." Bones said.

It took only a matter of minutes before they were all free. The knots were excellent, but far from impossible to work with two free hands.

Bones picked up Steve's gun and examined it before shoving it in his own waistband. "A Beretta. Not perfect but it could be worse."

Sterling glanced around the van, which was still illuminated by the flashlight. "So how do we get out of here?"

Maddock put a hand on the cart and allowed a smile to

gradually envelop his face.

"We wait for the van to slow down at a corner, and then we fly."

For just a second, the four-wheeler appeared to defy gravity as it launched out the back of the van. With the van traveling about forty-five miles an hour, Maddock knew the illusion would be short lived. He had no idea what would happen when they hit the pavement, and he mashed on the accelerator in an attempt to add stability.

The jolt was even worse than he could have imagined, the impact sending burning pain up his spine and down his limbs, but he knew it had to be harder on Bones, seated in the small bed on the back. Bones had wanted to drive out the back himself, but Maddock had won the day when he pointed out that the move was his idea. Sterling sat next to him, both buckled in with the most rudimentary of straps.

Now the cart bounced what felt like ten feet in the air but was probably no more than a few inches. Upon landing, it shifted onto only the left two tires, and Maddock threw himself across Sterling while wrenching the wheel to the right. This succeeded in regaining full contact with the ground, but at the expense of starting a spin.

He considered the standard advice to steer into a skid and concluded that the admonition never anticipated this maneuver. Instead he fell back on two far more instinctive actions. He slammed on the brake and prayed.

He had no idea which of the two was more critical, but the end result was that they came to a stop, still on the blacktop. They were facing back toward the disappearing Sprinter, which had not yet shown illuminated brake lights in the darkness. It was just possible that Jamison had no clue about the escape.

"Hang on."

He said this mostly for Bones' benefit as he did a one-eighty and accelerated. Step one was to put as much distance as a possible between himself and the van. Step two was find a decent size cross road to take. Then another one, to create more options for pursuit than Jamison could chase down. The cart appeared to have a top speed of about twenty-five, which is plenty fast on the golf course but death when trying to escape from one hundred-fifty horses of internal combustion.

Darkness was in their favor, though there were no streetlights so he couldn't turn off their lights entirely. He discovered a set of fog lights and used those instead. Fortune continued to smile on them, as he actually turned on three paved cross streets in succession over the course of about five miles. Rolling to a stop about fifty feet down a dirt road lined with trees, he felt that they were as safe as they could be under the circumstances.

Bones popped out of the back onto his feet and let out a whoop. "Man, *that* is what I call an adrenaline rush! We have got to try that again sometime. But I get to drive."

After multiple nights of no sleep combined with the recent adrenaline-laced escape, Maddock didn't have the energy to laugh.

"Okay Bones. Next time we propel a cart out the back of a moving vehicle, you drive."

"I'm gonna hold you to that." He turned to gaze down the darkened street. "I guess that's that. What do we do now?"

Maddock grinned. "The Sons might have the journal, but they don't have all of it."

Sterling frowned. "What are you talking about?"

"I took a page out of Billy Lee's playbook. Pun intended." He reached into his hip pocket and pulled out a folded sheet of paper.

Sterling folded her arms. "You didn't trust me." It wasn't a question.

"Don't take it personally. We've learned not to trust people."

The look in her eyes said that Sterling didn't find the answer satisfactory, but she kept her silence.

"I actually translated the last page before I worked on anything else, and it contains a clue I think is worth following."

"What's that?" Bones asked.

"We're going to find the *Queen Anne's Revenge*."

TWELVE

Edmonia Jennings Wright picked up the phone with some hesitation. She hated having to keep someone else informed. Her alliance with the individual on the other end of the line could never be a relationship of equals. Still, she was fully prepared to go it alone if the balance of power skewed any further in the wrong direction.

The phone rang and was answered on the other end.

"Hello, Edmonia."

Even the familiarity of the greeting served to highlight the power of the speaker. Wright had spent decades honing the ability to push aside irritation and even dissipate it the instant it appeared. No trace of frustration adorned her voice.

"I have a status update. We recovered the journal. It's in code, but that won't be a problem."

"Excellent. How long do you anticipate it will take to translate it?"

"Not long. The cipher is a common one used during the colonial period. I expect it will be complete in a few days at the most."

"Anything else?"

"Yes." She hesitated. "The two SEALs have escaped with the park policewoman."

The man on the other end paused. *"I thought you said you put your best man on it."*

"I did. He failed."

"Perhaps he needs replacing."

"Perhaps."

Another pause. *"Do I need to get more involved?"*

"That is of course up to you. This sort of endeavor never proceeds without setbacks. We have the journal, which is what matters most."

"You don't think your escapees will cause more problems?"

The emphasis on *your* grated at her nerves.

"Let them try. There's no way they had time to translate the entire journal, assuming they managed to break the code at all. If they want to continue the chase, they'll have to take it back from us, and that isn't going to happen."

"I have to go. Inform me the minute you have more information that gets us closer to the prize."

It was a typical ending to these conversations. Wright decided then and there only to make another call when discovery was imminent. Perhaps not even then.

Jamison's loss of Maddock and Bonebrake was disappointing, but she wouldn't be too hard on him. Men like Jamison were hard to come by, and disposing of everyone who made mistakes only sounded good in the movies and at Congressional hearings. The fact was that they had the journal, putting them one step closer to their goal.

Soon, her search would be at an end.

A single beam of golden light sliced through the dusty air in Hunter Maddock's private library and shone on the antique map spread out on the desk. Elizabeth never missed a chance to comment on this room's need for a thorough cleaning, but Hunter liked it this way. It reminded him of the old library he'd frequented as a child, devouring books like Treasure Island and Journey to the Center of the Earth. Besides, it was nice to allow himself one aspect of his life that wasn't shipshape and Bristol fashion.

His eyes drifted from the map to the framed photograph on his desk. He took out a handkerchief and brushed the dust from the glass. Three faces smiled back at him. Hunter, with fewer gray hairs; Elizabeth, looking as beautiful as the day they'd met; and Dane in his Full Dress uniform. As always, Hunter's chest swelled with pride at the thought of his son.

The phone rang, jolting him from his thoughts. As always, he picked up on the first ring.

"Hunter Maddock."

"Dad? How's it going?"

"Dane. I thought you were off mountain climbing with that…interesting friend of yours." Hunter still wasn't sure what to make of the big, roguish Cherokee whom his son had befriended. He had to admit, the man had a certain charm, and Dane vouched for him, so that was something.

"We were diverted."

Hunter thought he detected a note of hesitation in his son's voice.

"Is everything all right?"

"Fine," Dane said too quickly. "I wanted to ask you about your pirate research."

A chill ran down Hunter's spine, and for one irrational moment he wondered if Dane knew about… No, it was impossible.

"Are you still there?"

"Yes. I'm just surprised that you've finally taken an interest in treasure hunting."

Dane laughed. "Sort of. It's hard to explain." He cleared his throat. "I know Captain Kidd is your thing, but do you know much about Blackbeard?"

"How much time do you have?"

"Not much, though I'd be happy to hear all about it next time I'm home for a visit. What I'm specifically wondering is, do you have any idea where *Queen Anne's Revenge* went down?"

Now it was Hunter's turn to laugh. "You have caught the bug. Don't deny it. But the answer to your question is, yes, I have a very good idea where she lies."

"Really?"

Hunter smiled at the excitement in his son's voice.

"A private corporation believes it has pinpointed the wreck. I have it on good authority that the spot lies just off the shore of Fort Macon Park in Atlantic Beach, North Carolina. I can't be more specific than that, but word is, they've got people out there right now doing sonar scans and taking underwater photographs. They're trying to get enough documentation to justify permits and get funding."

"So, I find the researchers and I find the wreck. Thanks,

Dad. You're the best."

Hunter bade his son goodbye and hung up the phone. Once again he stared at the framed photograph. With a sigh, he took out his wallet, reached into a tiny compartment, and took out a photograph of a blonde-haired, blue-eyed girl.

"I ought to tell him," he whispered. "And I would if I were half the man he is."

THIRTEEN

Maddock allowed himself to relax completely as he dropped to the bottom of the ocean. The descent took only a few seconds, and he found both feet planted in a bed of rocks and sand. Switching on his headlamp, he spotted Bones a few feet away. They'd easily found the location. As his father had warned him, researchers buzzed around the area, but had left before sunset and hadn't returned.

The wreck of Blackbeard's flagship lay in less than thirty feet of water within sight of Atlantic Beach on the North Carolina coast. The alleged wreck, Maddock reminded himself. It wasn't likely to be certified as authentic for some time. But Maddock kept himself up to date about interesting shipwrecks, and everything he had seen told him that the ship was indeed the legendary *Queen Anne's Revenge.*

This would be one of the easiest dives he had ever undertaken. No need for decompression stops. No need for communication with the surface. The current near the surface was several knots, but down at the bottom he could stand without having to steady himself at all.

The main concern here was secrecy, which is why he hadn't switched on his light until now. They were exploring after midnight in a prescribed location. He didn't figure the archaeological team would be diving the wreck tonight, but the need to stay silent and dark remained. A SEAL specialty.

Sterling had no diving experience and remained on board the rowboat they had used to traverse the mile from the shore. A little exertion with the oars was a small price to pay for avoiding the tell-tale sounds of a motor. After dropping anchor, they had slipped over the side.

Bones motioned with his flashlight along a trench in the seabed. Maddock knew that a number of these trenches dotted the area, designed to assist in locating items which scattered when the ship struck bottom. Without some structure to the digging, over time the sea would defeat all attempts at methodical searches.

Their target was the ship itself. He didn't know what they would find, but he and Bones had one big advantage over the archaeologists: They didn't have to follow any defined safety rules when exploring the wreck. Neither man wanted to damage the site, nor did they want to meet a quick end from a falling timber. But they could swim through the wreck without any kind of detailed plan of action.

As they reached the hull, they glided over what had to be one of the cannons entombed in silt. The ship had settled in a generally upright position, though of course it leaned to one side. Maddock felt a sort of reverence as he settled just above a square opening in the deck and peered into darkness. He felt something similar any time he dived on an old wreck, imagining that doing something like this for a living after leaving the military would have great appeal.

The beam of Bones' light cut through the gloom, and Bones moved slowly into the opening head first. Maddock gave it about ten seconds after the big man's feet disappeared before following into another world.

Everything was covered with various forms of aquatic growth, but he could still see what was intact and what wasn't. Moving slowly, he made his way deeper into the ship through a couple of different openings. At one point he stopped and backtracked a few feet. He had almost missed a tiny container tucked under a collapsed beam. He opened it, discovering several coins inside. How could you beat diving on a pirate ship and finding a treasure chest? He shook off a twinge of guilt as he slipped the coins into his dive bag.

Some time later he spotted Bones' light. Closing the gap, both of them swum up through another opening to leave the interior of the wreck. Maddock looked at his watch and was only partially surprised to find that over thirty minutes had passed. He jerked his thumb upwards and Bones nodded.

He left his flashlight on during the short trip to the surface, but kept it pointing downward. A brief flick across the surface confirmed the location of the rowboat, and he switched it off for good. A few freestyle strokes saw him climbing smoothly over the side.

"Where's Bonebrake?"

"What's the matter, did you miss me?" Bones raised himself into the boat a moment later.

"No, but I'm going to miss the peace and quiet. Did you guys find anything?"

Bones shook his head, spraying brine in her face. "Just a few coins."

"So it was all for nothing, right? This was our final clue."

"I don't know," Maddock said. "There was no treasure, but I didn't get the feeling that the wreck had been plundered."

"Me neither," Bones said. "It's doesn't have that vibe."

"Vibe?" Sterling asked.

Bones winked. "Trust us. Besides, no one's ever been certain of the location of this wreck, and as far as I know, no treasure associated with Blackbeard has ever shown up."

Maddock looked at Bones, but even with a sliver of moon visible, he couldn't see enough to make eye contact in the darkness. "That gives me an idea. You and I both know someone who might be able to find out more about these coins."

"We do? Oh yeah, Jimmy Letson. We keep calling him every time we need research and we'll owe him so much Wild Turkey we'll need to buy stock in the company."

Sterling still didn't sound pleased. "Who the hell is Jimmy Letson?"

"He started SEAL training with me and Bones. Great guy, a genius with computers, but couldn't hack the physical side. He's now a reporter in DC. He was traveling when we first hit the area, but I'm pretty sure he got back yesterday. We'll show him the coins and see if he has any ideas."

Sterling just grunted in reply, which Maddock took as a sign that the discussion had ended. He settled himself into the center, set the oars in the locks, and started rowing.

He allowed himself to disappear into the repetitive motion, thinking about the coins. Letson would come up with something. He always did.

FOURTEEN

The last time he'd spoken with Jimmy Letson was in
Boston during their first run-in with the Sons of The
Republic. He had just started working for *The Globe*, and his
small apartment had the feel of post-collegiate geekdom.
Now Jimmy worked for the *Washington Post* and lived in
upscale Georgetown, something Maddock had a bit of
trouble reconciling with the man he knew.

Maddock and Bones had decided to make the drive
without Sterling, figuring her absence would make Letson
more comfortable about discussing information obtained via
hacking.

When the gangly, curly-haired Letson answered the
door, Maddock could tell immediately that his friend hadn't
changed, at least not in any way that really mattered. Jimmy
wore a brown t-shirt which read 'Who's Your Dungeon
Master?', and his jeans below mid-thigh sported barely
enough thread to maintain structural integrity. His eyes
didn't quite focus until Bones held up a bottle in a paper
bag.

"Is that. . ."

Bones grinned as Letson took the bag and opened it
with deliberate and careful movements. "Wild Turkey, my
friend. I hear you're a bourbon man, now."

Letson held the bottle below his large nose, the lip
brushing his thick, brown mustache. "You heard right.
Come on in."

Letson pressed a key on a keypad mounted just inside
the door, and then they followed him through a hallway into
a living room with simple but tasteful furniture. This was a
far cry from the thrift store motif at his place in Boston.

Bones slapped him on the shoulder. "Looks like making
the big bucks agrees with you. It almost looks like a
grownup lives here."

Maddock said, "Bones, I'm guessing it has more to do

with Jimmy's new girlfriend. Women aren't satisfied with crate tables, a beanbag chair, and early George Lucas for artwork."

Letson stopped and glared. "You wound me, Maddock. Lucas is a genius. Though you're right that Sheri assisted me with the decorating."

"How long have you two been dating?" Bones asked.

"About three months. So two months more than your longest relationship unless you've turned over a new leaf. She's into science fiction and computers, so I'm hoping we have a future together. Anyway, follow me."

Letson continued walking into another hallway. Maddock remembered Bones once saying he looked like Weird Al with his skinny frame and mass of curly hair, and he couldn't much argue with that assessment. Right down to the John Lennon glasses, which Letson didn't need but liked the look of. His skin was darker than last time, no doubt due to his recent trip to the Caribbean.

Letson directed them into a room which looked far more like Maddock had expected. With a cavernous ceiling and only two small lamps, shadows floated everywhere. The poster collection had expanded to include Indiana Jones in addition to Star Wars, which Maddock considered a definite step in the right direction. The clear focus of the space, however, was over half a dozen monitors and all manner of computers and peripheral equipment.

Bones let out a whistle. "Holy crap. Are you working for the government now?"

"Nah, these are just the tools of my trade. I'm actually making money on the side as a white hat."

"You mean like the guys in *Spy vs Spy*?"

Letson guffawed. "Those books were great, but no. A white hat is someone who gets hired by companies and organizations to use their hacking skills to test systems for vulnerabilities."

Maddock pondered this. "Sounds to me like there's an awfully blurry line there. You have to be good enough to break the law without getting caught, but ethical enough that they can trust you."

"You hit the nail on the head. It actually started when I found a major vulnerability in one of the commonly used network software packages. The company was grateful enough to hire me to attack them once a month and generate a report."

He sat down in front of the two largest monitors. Maddock looked at Bones, who shrugged before taking a seat next to the hacker. Letson had that combination of hyper-focus and spaciness so often found in technically oriented people.

"Okay, Mister Cloak-and-Dagger, what's so sensitive that you couldn't tell me about it over the phone?"

"It's something we wanted to show you." Maddock took out a plastic bag holding a worn gold coin. "We found this among the wreckage of *Queen Anne's Revenge*. Blackbeard's ship," he added, seeing Jimmy's puzzled expression.

Letson set to work immediately, scanning both sides Zippoand loading the images onto his computer. At least, that's what he told Maddock and Bones he was doing. Neither had any sort of computer expertise.

Letson's fingers flew over the keyboard so fast that Maddock couldn't possibly have said which letters he was keying. Window after window opened and closed on the monitor until finally an image appeared that he recognized: a picture of a worn gold coin exactly like the ones he had found on the *Queen Anne's Revenge*.

"Gentlemen, I think we have a winner!"

"That's it exactly," Maddock said. "You're incredible!"

"You said it, I didn't. How about this one? Did you find any like that?"

Another picture flashed on the screen, this time of a coin similar to one which Bones had found. "Hot damn, Letson, you are the man. How did you find those?"

When he swiveled his chair to face them, a triumphant smile graced his face. "I've told you before about the Internet. Someday everything ever known to man will be connected on one big network. By now, I'm sure you've learned enough to know I'm right. Finding the pictures was easy. The hard part will be finding out the significance of these specific coins."

He returned to the keyboard and pounded away. Maddock almost held his breath as he watched his old friend work.

Ten minutes later, Jimmy paused, sat back, and cracked his knuckles. "You said you found the coins at a shipwreck?"

"Previously undiscovered," Bones added.

"I'm sure your mom is very proud. Where was this wreck, exactly?"

"North Carolina."

"North Carolina," Jimmy whispered as he returned to typing. "It seems," he finally announced, "there are actually very few of these coins still in existence and you could probably sell yours for major bucks. Turns out, every coin like this one I could find came from the same place. Sound like useful information?"

Maddock knew Letson was enjoying stringing them along. "As long as that place wasn't off the coast of Atlantic Beach."

"Oh, it wasn't a ship." He paused for dramatic effect. "It was a cave in North Carolina."

FIFTEEN

"Hey Maddock, remember the time we got stuck in a cave and that bear chased us?"

"I also remember we agreed never to speak of it again. But there was another cave after that where we found something awesome, or have you forgotten already?"

Bones shook his head. "People carved that place so it doesn't count as a cave."

Sterling stared at them. "What the hell are you guys talking about?"

Maddock exchanged glances with Bones. "It's a long story. Bones, help me move this rock."

Maddock and Bones put their backs into the effort and the five-foot tall slab of granite slid eighteen inches to the side. The movement generated a scratching sound as it rubbed against the rock of the ground. Stepping aside, Maddock could now see an opening through which they could fit.

Bones rubbed his hands together. "Allow me to lead the way."

Maddock gestured with his hand in agreement. He, Bones, and Sterling had driven back into southern North Carolina to a spot about twenty miles inland from the wreck of the *Queen Anne's Revenge*. Jimmy Letson had given them the exact location of the cave where similar coins had been found, the cave which now beckoned.

Letson had not been able to find any pictures of the cave, just a brief summary about the discovery of the coins. The cave was on national forest land and the reports suggested that from time to time local youth would decide to bushwhack over a mile through dense scrub to reach it. Two teenagers had discovered a few dozen pieces of gold and silver about a decade earlier, and a period of several years with increased scrutiny followed. But no one found anything else, and activity had died down as far as Letson could tell.

They had no information about the size of the cave other than the fact that there were two chambers and it was tall enough in some spots for a man to stand. This fact alone made it unusual, but the remote location and disinclination of the federal government to allow any official exploration or development meant that no one except locals knew about it.

Jimmy Letson knew, Maddock reminded himself. One of these days they were going to have to give the guy something more than just a bottle of booze.

Bones paused before ducking his head through the opening. "Remember when we were out looking for Blackbeard's ghost a couple nights ago?"

"How could I forget?"

"Well, that feeling I had that we weren't alone? I have that same feeling right now. As we went through the woods, I saw a sign or two that something else walking on two legs had been in the area recently."

"Maybe it was Bigfoot." Sterling managed to deliver the line without humor.

"Nah, Bigfoot would have left bigger signs. Plus there's always a funky smell around Bigfoot."

"I was kidding, Bones."

"Never kid about Bigfoot." Bones displayed most of his teeth in a look Maddock couldn't describe as completely humorous. "That's okay, I'll let it slide this time. Anyway, we just need to be extra careful."

With that he disappeared into the cave. Maddock allowed Sterling to go next and he brought up the rear. All three carried MagLites and Glocks. Sterling had grudgingly provided them with the weapons. The Lieutenant had definitely loosened up somewhat after the initial day or two, probably because they were getting closer to finding the treasure.

The initial chamber was roughly circular, about fifteen feet in diameter, with walls seemingly chiseled from the stone. About four feet into the room, the ceiling rose high enough for Maddock to stand without bending at all.

He noticed surprisingly little moisture on the rocky surfaces and the whole picture made him wonder how such a place could have been created. Water was the only force likely to have done this, but normally that left behind plenty of small channels for ingress and egress, which would have rendered the cave overgrown in short order.

Slowly they moved through an opening on the far side of the room, this one requiring them to get on their knees and crawl through. Maddock didn't feel like they had searched the initial chamber fully, but he figured Bones wanted to take in the bigger picture before beginning more methodical work. The second chamber was much like the first except about half the diameter, with a maximum ceiling height of about five feet. Unlike the first room, which was clear of pretty much everything, this one contained a number of scattered rocks ranging from pebbles to slabs three or four feet long.

They searched for half an hour, inspecting every inch of the surface. They poked, prodded, and pushed until they finally were forced to admit defeat.

"What now?" Bones asked.

"Maybe go have a beer and regroup," Maddock said, tucking his MagLite in his pocket as they stepped out into the sun.

"Hold on! You're just giving up?" Sterling stood at the cave entrance with her hands on her hips. "We can't do that."

"We're not giving up, but we need a new plan. Obviously, the cave is a dead end." Maddock sighed. "Maybe the treasure was with the wreck and Washington did manage to retrieve it somehow."

"But if that were the case, he'd have left instructions for Lafayette to find it," she argued. "Otherwise, what would be the point of leaving him the journal?"

Maddock came to a sudden stop. "You're right." He quickened his pace, forcing even the long-legged Bones to double-time it.

"What's the deal, Maddock?" Bones asked.

"Maybe nothing. We'll see."

"Cryptic might work for books and movies, but in real life it's a big pain in the butt, you know that?"

"So are you."

"Touché."

When they reached the car, Maddock grabbed the cipher book in which he had placed the last page of Washington's journal, along with the translation.

"The last page of the journal had only part of a single line." He held up the page.

...there you will find the wreck of the Queen Anne's Revenge.

"When I read it, I naturally assumed the *Revenge* would be the end of the journey. But, like Sterling says, if that's the case, it doesn't make sense that Washington would make this the last clue." He looked at Bones. "Can I borrow your Zippo?"

Bones understood immediately. "If you're right about this, drinks are on me tonight."

"If I'm right, we might be too busy to go for drinks." He popped open the lid of the Zippo and an instant later, flame blossomed in the deep forest shade. Carefully, he held it under the page—close enough to warm it but not so close as to scorch the aged paper.

"Now I don't know if I want you to be right or not," Bones said. "I really could go for a beer."

They didn't have to wait long to find out. In a matter of seconds, dark lines appeared on the page.

"There's more to the cipher!" Sterling gasped. "I'll copy it down."

"Sorry Bones," Maddock said with a grin. "I guess drinks will have to wait."

SIXTEEN

Turn your back to the rising sun.
Let your path be true.
Beyond the whispering waters.
Above the blackness so foul.
Into the mouth of the devil.
The disciples.
The days of creation.
The blessed trinity.
There was found that which pierced the flesh of our Savior.
May God have mercy on me.

"That's...not very specific." Sterling ran a hand through her hair. "Why couldn't he just say, *walk that way?*"

"He did," Maddock said. "Turn your back to the rising sun. That means face west."

"Let your path be true means… walk straight ahead?" Bones offered.

Sterling's expression brightened. "And there's a stream not too far from here. That could be the whispering water."

Maddock nodded. "That's enough to get us started. I guess we'll find out what the rest means as we go."

Beginning from the shore, due west of the wreck site, they began their march inland. The going quickly grew rough as the foliage grew dense. Palmettos, vines, and shrubs stood in their path, and Bones seemed to take their interference as a personal affront. The big native hacked and slashed at them, roughly clearing a path for his companions to follow.

"I'll bet you were a heck of a football player," Sterling said.

"Might have been, but I had a habit of getting kicked off of whatever team I joined."

"There's a shocker." Sterling winced as a branch Bones had pushed aside snapped back, cracking her across the cheek. "Did you do that on purpose?"

"Of course not. My humor is more sophisticated than that."

Sterling flashed her middle finger at Bones' back.

"I saw that," Bones said.

Sterling turned to Maddock. "How does he…?"

"It's a gift. No one can explain it."

They crossed the stream and continued on. The way grew steeper and they found themselves climbing a gentle slope.

"Man, what is that smell?" The words had barely escaped Bones' lips when the big man let out a cry and vanished from sight.

"Bones!" Maddock rushed forward but halted as he reached the edge of steep drop-off. Down below, Bones sat in several inches of black mud and stagnant water.

"I think I found the 'blackness so foul'." Bones crinkled his nose at the stench.

Maddock struggled to suppress his laughter, but failed miserably. Sterling slumped against his shoulder, tears of mirth streaming down her cheeks, her chest heaving.

"Joke's on you guys," Bones said. "If we're going to head due west, we're going to have to cross this…marsh, or whatever it is."

That got their attention. Maddock regained his composure with a few steadying breaths. Sterling, her shoulders still bobbing with silent laughter, scrubbed her cheeks.

"Actually," she gasped, "we're right at the edge. Maddock and I can circle it. Since you're already dirty, you might as well keep going straight ahead. We'll meet you there."

Now it was Bones' turn to flash an obscene gesture as Maddock and Sterling rounded the quagmire while Bones trudged onward. When they met on the other side, Bones' countenance was as dark as Maddock had ever seen it.

"Come on, Bones. It's just a little mud."

"It's not that. Look where we are."

Maddock followed his friend's line of sight and cursed at what he saw. "We're back at the cave."

"Oh, come on!" Sterling stamped her foot.

"Maybe it's not a bad thing," Maddock said. "We're back but now we have clues."

"So, if the cave is the 'mouth of the devil', then we need to go back inside and look for disciples." Skepticism hung heavy in Bones' words.

"Unless the cave isn't what we're looking for." As they strode up the gentle slope toward the cave, he scanned the surrounding area for anything that could be the mouth of the devil. When they reached the cave mouth, he paused. "I've got an idea. Sterling, how about you take a second look at the cave and see if there's something we missed that could fit the clues. Bones and I will look for anything else that might be called a devil's mouth."

Sterling frowned. "Why don't one of you check the cave and I'll keep searching?"

"We can do it that way, but if we want to keep going due west, there's going to be some climbing involved. No offense, but Bones and I will be able to go a lot faster on our own."

"And I could go even faster without Maddock," Bones chimed in.

Sterling eyed the steep, rocky cliff above the cave. "All right. But don't go too far without me. We need to remain within earshot in case one of us finds something." With that, she headed back to the cave while Maddock and Bones inspected the cliff face for hand and footholds.

"Do you have a plan or is this just a shot in the dark?" Bones said quietly.

"I have an idea. It's hard to tell with all the brush growing out of the cliff, but if it were clear, don't you think the formation above that ledge looks like the face of the devil?" He pointed to an odd formation thrusting out about ten meters above their heads. Over the years, wind and rain had smoothed the surface, but it was easy to make out what might have been a nose, eye sockets, a forehead, and horns.

"Might be the devil," Bones agreed. "Looks more like that chick Professor brought home last weekend."

Maddock grinned. Pete "Professor" Chapman was a fellow SEAL with less than exacting taste in women.

They made the climb in a matter of minutes. The going was easy and they soon found themselves standing on the ledge, looking at the rock formation.

"Doesn't look like the devil from up here," Bones said, "and I don't see a mouth."

"Look closer." Maddock pushed back a thick shrub. "What do you see?"

"The wall isn't solid." Bones brushed the surface with his fingertips. "Someone did a good job fitting these blocks together, but you can see the seams."

"And the holes they plugged up with mud." Maddock smiled. "I assume you want to do the honors?"

"You know it." Bones stood and attacked the wall with a vicious arsenal of martial arts kicks until, finally, one of the stones broke loose. He and Maddock worked it free, revealing an open space behind it.

"So there *is* a cave here," Maddock said.

"Good call." Bones cast an appraising look at him. "You know, you do just enough things right for me to keep you around."

"Thanks," Maddock deadpanned. "I'll let you finish the job while I get Sterling."

By the time Maddock and the agent arrived, Bones had cleared a space large enough for a person to squeeze through. Bones glanced at Sterling. "Ladies first?"

"Really?" Sterling smiled.

"Sure. In case it's booby trapped." Bones flashed a roguish grin that Sterling returned with a smirk.

"You're a gem, you know that?"

"Just messing with you. Big dude goes first. That way we know you little people can make it through." He flicked on his MagLite, stuck it in his teeth, turned, and plunged headfirst through the hole.

Sterling shook her head. "If he gets stuck, can we just

leave him here?"

"I would, but I'm a little scared of his sister."

Sterling made a face. "I can't even imagine what that would look like."

"Don't get me wrong," Maddock hurried on. "She's actually really cute, she's just… vicious." His thoughts suddenly filled with images of Bones' sister. Angel, her big, brown eyes, her long hair held back in tight braids, pulverizing a punching bag with a flurry of punches and kicks. The young woman was fast becoming a legend in the local mixed martial arts scene. She was also modeling on the side, and Maddock found the juxtaposition of her two careers bizarre.

"Your face is a dozen shades of red." Sterling arched an eyebrow.

"Oh! I was just thinking of something else."

Bones voice interrupted them. "All right, you two. Get in here."

Sterling and Maddock clambered through the hole. They had to crawl for a short distance before standing.

"You got something?" Maddock asked.

"Maybe." Bones started moving his hands over the ground as Maddock and Sterling moved closer. His hands bumped up against the wall and stopped. He moved the flashlight back and forth before slowing down along what was now visible as a vertical seam in the stone wall. "It doesn't fit any of the clues, but it's definitely not natural."

Sterling added her light to his, catching a horizontal seam extending from the top of the vertical one about five feet off the ground, and then another vertical seam parallel to the first. "That's not natural. Is that a door?"

"I don't know if it swings like a door, but we can try pushing."

Maddock grabbed his shoulder. "Hold on, Bones. Booby traps, remember?"

Bones grimaced. "Okay, what do we do, then?"

"First we look around for any sort of lever or handle that might open it. But we just look at it, we don't touch it."

Sterling said, "It could be anywhere in here."

Bones nodded. "In the movies, they never put it right next to the door. That would be too easy."

She looked at him. "Is that what they did in Boston?" She was fishing.

"Boston was something else entirely. You know, we could have dinner sometime and I'll tell you all about it."

"I may regret this, but I'll tell you what. If we find this treasure and stop the Sons of The Republic, you're on."

Bones rubbed his hands together. "Awesome! I knew you'd eventually come around. How about we break the room into thirds and start searching?"

For the next thirty minutes, they did just that, switching sections when they each finished their initial third. By the time they were done, each of them had actually searched the top, bottom and sides of the cave in its entirety. They found nothing.

Bones flopped to the floor near the supposed door. "What now?"

Maddock shone his light on the seams. "I'm thinking."

Sterling said, "I have an idea. Maybe we're making this too complicated. Maybe that's just a big stone and we push it and it moves."

Bones rallied himself to his hands and knees. "Hey, you could be onto something. Maddock here's going to tell us it's too dangerous, though."

Maddock scanned the rest of the room with the light. "How about this? We take a couple of those larger rocks on the floor, put one on top of the other, then one of us lies on the ground and pushes with his feet."

Bones raised his hand. "I volunteer. I can probably reach my arms all the way to the wall so I'll have major leverage."

A minute later they were ready. Bones lay on his back with both hands over his head and touching one wall. His feet touched the two three-foot long rocks they had placed in front of the door. The rocks were essentially rectangular and fortunately had settled right into the desired positions without much wobbling. Sterling had backed into the entrance to the room, while Maddock lay just in front of her, ready to lunge toward Bones to pull him out if needed.

"Whenever you're ready, Bones."

Bones started to straighten his legs and exert pressure. Maddock moved his flashlight back and forth between the seams and Bones, and he didn't detect any sign of movement. Bones' face was a mask of concentration and exertion.

After about fifteen seconds, he stopped and sucked in a few deep breaths.

"You okay, Bones?"

"Hell yes, I'm just getting warmed up. That was like five hundred pounds on the leg press machine. Time to raise it to seven-fifty."

The second time, the stones still weren't moving. Maddock thought Bones would have to take another break, but then an ear-shattering roar split the air. It took Maddock a second to realize that it had come from Bones. The sound reminded him of a martial arts *keop*, but with a deeper tone that sounded far more ominous and seemed to shake the earth. Maddock couldn't be sure about the latter, because a split second later the stones moved.

He and Sterling both flashed their lights onto the seams at the same time. They saw that the space had opened a few feet, revealing another wall.

Bones stood and cracked his knuckles. "You're welcome. What are you girls waiting for?"

Sterling leaned forward. "I think we're looking for the combination to this lock."

SEVENTEEN

"I don't see anything here." Wright shone her light around the empty chamber. This place was supposed to be the hiding place of the treasure, according to her source, but she saw nothing.

"Maddock and his friends were here," Ransom said. "We spotted their vehicle parked on the side of the road, and some of those footprints outside were too big to belong to anyone other than Bonebrake."

"Yet I neither see Misters Maddock and Bonebrake, nor Agent Sterling." She turned her light on Ransom and shone it directly in his eyes. It was a petty action, borne of frustration, but she took a measure of satisfaction as the man raised his arm and turned his head to the side.

"They have to have gone somewhere," she said.

"A secret room?" Ransom offered.

"Possibly, but I have yet to see anything that looks like a hidden door. Have you?"

Ransom shook his head.

"Keep up the search," she instructed. "I'll see what I can find."

She closed her eyes again, trying to let go of any specific thoughts of what else to do. She imagined her thoughts were corporeal, fingers that could reach out and brush the stone walls, seeking out every nook and cranny. In her mind's eye, she scanned the cave, feeling for an opening, for something hidden. Seconds passed, but nothing.

Dark thoughts began to intrude on her calm. Why did her search seemed doomed to failure? This was her destiny. She was the heir of Joan of Arc, by blood and spirit. Fate had chosen her to discover the existence of that greatest of treasures, and she would not be deterred.

She took a deep, cleansing breath, refocused her thoughts, only to have them shattered again as an ear-splitting shout pierced the air.

"It's some sort of combination lock." Maddock shone his light on four brass dials set in the wall. Each displayed a number. "We put in the four-digit combination and we're in."

"This can't be right," Sterling said. "I don't believe Blackbeard could have constructed something like this."

"No, but the Templars could have," Bones said. "A pirate captain could have learned the location of a Templar vault."

Sterling turned and fixed him with a flat stare. "Don't even try to foist your conspiracy theories on me. Templar vaults in the New World? Save it for a cable TV show."

Bones flashed a knowing grin at Maddock, who winked. They knew a little something about Templars and their treasures.

Sterling gaped. "Is this another thing you two aren't going to tell me? Oh my God! I hate it when you do that."

"Not now, anyway," Maddock said.

"Fine, how about we get to work on this combination?"

"Work?" Bones said. "This one's child's play. Even I figured it out."

"Oh really?" Sterling said. "Enlighten us, then."

"Think about the clues. There were twelve disciples, seven days of creation, and the Trinity is three."

"Hmmm…" Sterling tapped her chin thoughtfully. "Makes sense to me." She spun the dials setting them to 1-2-7-3.

Nothing.

"I guess you were wrong," Sterling said.

"I think he's on the right track," Maddock said. "Remember, on the seventh day, God rested. Six days of creation." He reached out and turned the third dial a single click.

With a deep rumble, the wall slid down until it disappeared into the floor.

"Typical Maddock," Bones said. "I do ninety-nine percent of the work and he swoops in and gets all the credit." The big man moved through the gap in the wall.

Sterling followed with Maddock bringing up the rear. All three had to duck their heads, as the top of the stone which had shifted was a few inches under five feet tall. Maddock floated his flashlight in a sweeping move across the space they had entered.

The walls and floor were cracked and pitted, speaking of great age. Water dripped down every surface, pooling in places and draining into the fractures beneath their feet. Carved vaults lined the far wall, empty save a layer of detritus at the bottom of each.

"There's no treasure," Bones said.

"It was probably here at one time." Sterling moved to the closest vault, knelt, and sifted through the debris. "I found a few coins," she called. "Like the ones you brought up from the wreck. I guess some fell through the cracks in the floor and ended up in the cave down below." She paused. "I'm going to keep looking." With that, she disappeared deeper into the vault.

"I guess this is the end of the road, Maddock." Bones clapped him on the shoulder.

Maddock didn't reply. His attention was fixed on a something to their left—a skeleton lying atop a slab. They moved toward the remains and Bones whistled.

"Is this Blackbeard?" Bones asked.

Maddock pointed to a single word carved in the wall.

TEACH

"It's him. I guess the legends about his death weren't true." The damp environment had not been kind to the remains of the legendary pirate, if, in fact that was who lay here. Most of the flesh had rotted away, leaving only bits of cloth and the moldering remains of leather boots to cover the man's bones. A few stringy bits of black hair stubbornly clung to the skull, along with patches of the once-ample beard where the fearsome pirate had tied smoking tapers to give himself a more fearsome appearance in battle. At his side lay a sword in a scabbard.

"This doesn't look like your typical pirate sword." Bones picked it up and slid the blade back, exposing a fine blade with five crosses engraved in the surface.

Five crosses! Maddock's heart leaped. "Turn it over."

Bones flipped the blade over and Maddock leaned forward. There, gleaming dully in the light, was the word *JUSTICE*.

"This is Joan of Arc's sword!"

"I didn't know she had a special sword," Bones said.

"It depends on which legend you stumble across. Most agree that she found the sword buried behind the altar of a church called St. Catherine's. It was covered in rust, but she claimed that it cleaned easily, almost miraculously. And when she cleaned it, she saw the five crosses on the blade. She called the sword 'Justice' and one of her followers had the name engraved upon it."

"It looks like it's never been used." Bones drew the blade the rest of the way out of the scabbard and held it up for inspection.

"It probably wasn't. She was a leader, a strategist, and a symbol, but not really a fighter. She didn't engage in combat..." Maddock broke off as something fell out of the scabbard and fluttered to the ground. A folded piece of paper.

Carefully, he picked it up and unfolded it.

"What is it?" Bones asked.

"A letter...from Blackbeard."

EIGHTEEN

December 25, 1718

The cold has added its burden to my grievous wound and I'll not see the morrow. This room which has served me in life will provide my tomb. A man could do far worse.

The two swords should have finished me, but somehow I surfaced from the fall. When I finally washed ashore, word of my death had already spread. Truth be told I felt more dead than alive. Hiding in my cave to await my recovery seemed the wise course. I learned of the legend of the cave years ago and, upon finding it, knew it could serve as an occasional retreat from the forces intent on my capture. It served one additional purpose which I will describe presently.

My expected recovery has been the opposite. The pus and blood in my neck is now a demon intent on snatching my soul. I will be free of it before the next sunrise. Or so I speculate, as I have not seen a sunrise in over a week. So be it.

I only hope I can finish this entry before I meet my final end, an end which I can only guess targets the inferno. Think not that in my final moments I am attempting to make amends. It is far too late for that. Still, there is no purpose in taking my knowledge to the grave.

It was but a year ago that I captured La Concorde near the Isle of Saint Vincent. Such a large guineaman was a prize indeed and I determined at once to rename it Queen Anne's Revenge and re-purpose it as my flagship. I discovered its real value later.

The ship had originally departed from France before taking on the cargo of slaves in Africa. The captain bore the markings of the ancient order and it is for that reason I know the treasure I found in his cabin to be genuine. Indeed, the very sight of it pierced my heart as it once pierced sacred flesh, and righteous fear froze my blood. I had only to touch it to realize it was an object which commanded great reverence. The fates were guarding me that day, protecting my find from the wild eyes of my men until I secured it.

I came to believe it a gift to me, a source of power and good fortune. Now that the failures have compounded, I consider that it was the opposite. In any case, I have told not a soul about it, nor even mentioned it in this journal until now.

The object is contained in a quite ordinary wooden box. Strange that such an item should rest in such a simple vessel, but our Lord came to us as a simple man, so mayhap it is fitting. Perhaps it deserves a better resting place, but it will rest with me in my chosen place. Providence brought this treasure to me and perhaps, some day, that same providence will bring this journal, or this treasure, to a worthier man. Or maybe it will remain a mystery for eternity. I will not be there to see it.

E Teach

Maddock didn't say a word when he finished reading the final pages of the journal. Bones, looking over his shoulder, wasn't so reticent.

"I was right. Blackbeard survived the fight. Even I wasn't going to buy that he swam around a ship three times without a head. This totally rocks."

Dizzy with the thrill of discovery, Maddock absently turned the page over and was surprised to see a single line of text.

This treasure I will take to my grave. G Washington

The word "grave" was written in larger letters than the rest of the sentence, and underlined.

"Son of a…" Bones said. "Washington did get here first. He took the treasure. Or treasures, I guess I should say, because I don't see a wooden box anywhere."

"That's all right," a voice said from behind them. "I know where to look. Now, hands in the air."

Maddock's first instinct was to fight, but he knew the situation was hopeless. There was nowhere to take cover and to go for his weapon would be suicide. Slowly he turned to face Edmonia Jennings Wright. Flanked by two of her men, they all held weapons trained on Maddock and Bones.

Maddock glanced at his friend and the two of them slowly raised their hands above their heads.

"You, Bonebrake," Wright snapped. "Put the sword and the paper back into the scabbard and toss it over to me. I don't need to tell you what will happen if I even think you're about to try something."

Glowering, Bones complied with her instructions, pitching the aged weapon in a slow arc, softball style, to the old woman. Had there been fewer weapons trained on them, Maddock might have been tempted to draw his weapon and start firing while all eyes were on the sword, but Wright was too wily for that. Her gun never lowered and her eyes never left the two SEALS as she snatched the sword with her free hand.

"Very good. Ransom," she said to one of her men, "disarm them."

"How did you find us?" Bones asked as Wright's man relieved him and Maddock of their pistols and knives.

Wright chuckled. "The two of you have done a remarkable job of confounding my plans. I fear your success has caused you to underestimate me and my resources." She fell silent, her thin-lipped smile indicating that was the only answer she was going to provide.

"If you know where the treasure is, why are you here at all?" Bones continued. "Were you after the sword? Is it the real treasure?"

"I thought you were smarter than that," Wright said. "Not a great deal smarter, mind you. Think about it. The mention of our Lord, piercing sacred flesh, contained in a simple wooden box. The esteem with which Blackbeard and Washington both held it."

Maddock understood. "You're after the Crown of Thorns."

"Very good. I'd heard you were the intelligent one, relatively speaking."

"Yeah, but I'm the good-looking one," Bones said.

"What could the Sons of the Republic possibly want with a religious artifact? You're a political group." Maddock was buying time. Sterling was hiding in one of the vaults, and he hoped she was waiting for Wright and her men to lower their guards.

Wright clucked in disapproval. "You have no imagination. The truth is, someone else wants it—a powerful ally. He believes the discovery of the crown, proof that the Gospel is true, will lend authority to proper-thinking men and women in government, will undermine the Godless, and will enthrall the populace. It will smooth the path for the advancement of our agenda and expand our ally's already formidable power."

"And the politicians who aren't swayed by the crown?" Maddock asked. "You'll buy them off with Blackbeard's treasure, I suppose."

Wright shrugged. "Different incentives for different people."

"So, is this over?" Bones asked. "You say you know where the treasure is, you've got the sword, so you're good to go. All we wanted was to bring this to an end so you'd leave us and Maddock's girlfriend alone."

"I wish I could believe you," Wright said. "But we both know the two of you have been thorns in my side for too long. Pun intended."

Maddock knew the moment had come. "Lights," he whispered to Bones, so softly that he wondered if his friend would hear.

As Wright steadied her aim, Maddock dropped hard to the ground, smashing his MagLite as he hit the stone floor. Bones did the same, and darkness blanketed the chamber as the sound of gunshots thundered through the confined space.

In the strobe-like light of muzzle flare, Maddock saw Sterling shooting from the protection of an empty vault. He saw Wright's men turn and run, the old woman following suit a moment later. Sterling fired off another shot and then silence filled the room.

"Are you alive?" Her voice scarcely registered above the ringing in Maddock's ears.

"I'm okay," Maddock said.

"I'm good," Bones rumbled a moment later. "But I

think I ripped my jeans. She'll pay for that one."

"Do we go after them?" Sterling asked. "I thought about trying to get them when they crawled out of the cave, but there are three of them and only one of me."

"You did the right thing," Maddock said as Sterling flipped on her MagLite. "We're outgunned and I doubt you have much ammo left. Let's just try to get out of here alive and then we'll see if we can't beat them to the treasure."

"How are we going to do that?" Bones asked. "We don't know where it's hidden."

Maddock smiled.

"Actually, I think I know exactly where it is."

NINETEEN

Twin obelisks flanked the wrought iron gates that barred the entrance to the tomb. Like miniature versions of the famed monument that stood at the center of the National Mall, they shone in the moonlight with an ethereal glow.

Wright paced back and forth, filled with scarcely contained impatience, as Ransom worked at the lock. Nearby, Jamison kept an eye out for security. She was convinced her men could handle whatever came their way, but she preferred they do this without bloodshed.

And then there was the specter of Maddock and Bonebrake, always looming just over the horizon. She was convinced the men had not given up, and regretted not having killed them when she had the chance. She knew better than to play with her food before eating it.

"I've got it," Ransom whispered. He took a moment to spray lubricant on the hinges of the gate before giving it a push. It swung open with barely a hiss, and Wright led the way forward. The tomb lay in a marble vault beneath a brick archway. The entire brick façade of the structure loomed dark and forbidding, a bloody reddish-brown in the faint light. She glanced up at the stone tablet that hung above the archway. A beam of silver moonlight shone on the words engraved there.

Within this Enclosure Rest the remains of Gen'l George Washington

A chill ran down her spine. She stood literally feet away from the prize. Inside the crypt lay two marble sarcophagi: the final resting places of Martha and George Washington. And somewhere here, the treasure was hidden.

Ransom opened the gate and held it for Wright to enter first. She felt like a queen taking her throne as she stepped inside. The moment was here.

"Open them up," she ordered. "Start with Washington. He took the treasure to his grave, so I expect it to be here."

Ransom winced, but set to work immediately with the aid of his companions. Wright moved back to the arched entrance and gazed up at the moonlight. She would remember this night forever.

"Do you think you can pick this lock, Bones? It's pretty old." They stood before a heavy wooden door set in the crumbling, ivy-draped wall of Mount Vernon's so-called "Old Vault" or "Old Tomb" on the bank of the Potomac River. Maddock had gambled that Wright would not be aware that Washington's first intended resting place was, in fact, this aged family vault, originally constructed at the behest of his brother, Lawrence Washington.

So far, so good. Knowing that the Sons would likely be covering the roads and gates, they'd come by canoe, keeping close to shore, and then crept uphill through the forest cover until they reached the vault. On the way up, Bones had scouted the New Tomb and spotted the approach of Wright and her men. So it was a race. Could Maddock, Bones, and Sterling find the treasure before Wright and the Sons discovered their mistake and learned of the Old Tomb.

"Seriously, Maddock? You really think that motivates me?" Bones knelt, fished a few tiny implements from his pocket, and set to work.

"What does motivate you, anyway?" Sterling asked.

"The love of a challenge and the joy of making mayhem." He grinned, his straight white teeth shining in the moonlight, as the door swung open.

"Impressive," Sterling said. "Products of a misspent youth, I take it?"

"Products of an awesomely fun youth. But I'll tell you about it later."

They stepped inside and closed the door behind them, so as not to draw the attention of security. This was actually a low risk, as the minimal roving patrols at Mount Vernon never came by the old tomb. Guards would only pass within a quarter mile of their location two or three times the entire night.

In the course of their research, Maddock had come across the results of a seismological analysis that suggested the existence of half a dozen caves or open spaces beneath the grounds of the Mount Vernon estate. One of these spots lay near the side wall of Washington's old tomb, providing the obvious place to search for a hidden treasure. He really didn't have any sense of how far down the open space was, or its size. The survey showed some space, but not anything really defined.

The cool air inside the old crypt smelled of mold. Maddock shone his light around, revealing crumbling brick walls, but no sign of a trapdoor or entrance to a hidden treasure vault.

"Do we do this the slow way or the noisy way?" Bones asked.

"Noisy. Hand me the sledgehammer." Maddock hefted the heavy tool and gave it a swing. His first blow thudded on stone. Maybe not as loud as he had feared, but still a risk. He put the concern out of his mind and resumed the task at hand. Sterling held a flashlight while Bones kicked away debris after every stroke. Behind the brick wall lay a thick slab of mortar that crumbled and cracked with each stroke, reverberating with hollow thuds that promised open space beyond. Soon he had created a hole three feet across.

Bones poked his head through and shone his light into the opening.

"It looks like an old root cellar. Must have fallen into disuse and been covered over."

Maddock's shoulders sagged. "So I was wrong."

Bones popped his head back out of the hole. "Just messing with you. There's a shaft with metal rungs leading down. I think we've found it."

Sterling clenched her fists. "Can I shoot him now? Please?"

"Not yet. We'll need him in a fight."

Maddock took out his MagLite and peered into the hole. The shaft appeared to be no more than eight feet deep, and below it a short drop to a stone floor. He caught sight of a shape which might have been a body, but he couldn't be certain. Heart racing, he clambered through the hole in the wall, stepped over to the shaft, and tested the first rung.

Rust pitted its surface, but it didn't give. Gingerly, hands braced on either side of the shaft, he tried the next rung. It held too. Emboldened, he worked his way down. The iron was like ice beneath his grip, the surface rough. The dank, moldy smell was stronger here, but he scarcely noticed, intoxicated by the thrill of discovery.

When he reached the bottom rung, he dropped down to the floor and swung the light back and forth. A skeleton clad in the remains of colonial garb, a uniform by the look of it, lay sprawled at an awkward angle in one corner. As much as he wanted to stop and examine it, he owed it to Bones and Sterling to call them down. He yelled up to them.

"Bones, send Sterling down, and then come down yourself. If it seems like the rungs won't support your weight, don't take the chance. Otherwise all three of us will be stuck here."

"Are you calling me fat?" Bones asked.

"Yes. Now get down here."

"Roger that."

In no time, the three of them stood in the chamber. Looking up at the ceiling, they spotted a wooden trap door in a spot which would have led into the old tomb if actually opened.

Sterling shook her head. "Wow, whoever covered that up did a great job. If you go in the old tomb, there is no sign of the floor being repaired."

Maddock nodded. "Washington must have completely redone the floor to obscure their real intention. That way no one would stumble onto the treasure." He shone his light past the skeleton and into the open space beyond. "Speaking of treasure, let's see what we can find."

TWENTY

"There's nothing here." Ransom's voice trembled as he delivered the news to Wright. "We've checked both sarcophagi. They're solid, just like the floor underneath. No sign of hollow spaces, trapdoors, or anything, and certainly no lock where you could use that." He indicated the copy of the Bastille key hanging from Wright's belt.

Wright gritted her teeth. It had to be here somewhere. Nothing else made sense. "Everyone quiet." Her men obeyed immediately. Wright closed her eyes, found her center, and reached out, searching…

…and finding nothing.

"You told me you had things under control, Edmonia." A deep, resonant voice filled the crypt.

Edmonia opened her eyes and turned to face the last man on earth she wanted to see right now.

"What are you doing here?"

"I wanted to be here when you found it. Of course, I believed you when you said you knew where the treasure was hidden. I've risked exposure for nothing."

She forced herself to remain calm. "It's not for nothing. We're just missing something here."

The man folded his arms. "I think it's clear what we're missing. The treasure."

"Excuse me, Ms. Wright. I think I can help." Jamison stood just outside the entrance, his weapon trained on a trembling man in a security guard's uniform.

"Make it fast," she snapped.

"Tell them what you told me," Jamison said to the nervous man.

"This… this isn't the only tomb. The Wa-Washingtons were buried in the old vault and then moved here later."

"The old vault?" Wright felt her cheeks grow warm and hoped the near-darkness hid her embarrassment. She'd never heard of the old vault, so she'd had no reason to look anywhere other than this tomb. Of course, that didn't make her look any better in front of one of the most powerful men in the nation.

He fixed her with a condescending smile. "It looks like dumb luck is on your side, Edmonia. And a good thing, too. My patience is exhausted."

Wright ignored him. She strode over to the captive guard, her eyes boring into his.

"Show me."

"What's up with this skeleton?" Bones asked. "Washington wouldn't leave a man down here to die, would he?"

"Doesn't seem very presidential, does it?" Maddock mused. "Then again, neither was what he did to Billy Lee."

They moved closer to the skeleton. Seeing it up close, Maddock realized something was wrong. The grinning skull didn't look like it was made of bone. Nor did the bony fingers which clutched a small box. The thing looked as if it were carved from wood and painted white. And then Maddock realized the thing was clad in the scarlet uniform of the British. This was all wrong.

"What is that?" Sterling leaned over to take the box from the faux skeleton's dead hands.

"Sandra, no!" Maddock dove forward and knocked Sterling to the side as three iron spikes shot out of the wall.

"Oh my God," Sterling gasped as she looked up at the sharp points. "That's right where I was standing."

"You're all right. That's what matters." Bones hauled Maddock and Sterling to their feet. "I'm guessing that box is a red herring." He frowned. "You know, Washington was kind of an ass, wasn't he? I mean, he sent Lafayette all the way down to the cave only to come back here again, and then he left this booby trap."

Maddock ran his fingers through his hair. "I have a feeling he intended to add the final instructions to the journal but didn't get to it before he died. Maybe the letter to Lafayette was all he could manage. And the British uniform would have served as a warning to Lafayette, who hated the English."

Sterling nodded. "Agreed. So the hunt continues."

"Actually," Bones said, "I think the hunt is over." He pointed behind Maddock, who turned to see dozens of wooden chests piled haphazardly against the wall. Most lay open. The chests at the bottom had shattered from decay and pressure. All appeared empty.

"The treasure?" Sterling said.

"Gone," Maddock said. "And I don't mean taken to another place."

"I can't believe it." Bitterness laced Sterling's words. "After all we've been through, there's nothing left?"

"Maybe one thing." The beam of Maddock's light had fallen on a simple wooden box sitting in an alcove. Beneath it lay an oilcloth pouch. Above the box, a soldier carved in the wall stood watch.

"Is that it? The Crown of Thorns?" Sterling whispered.

"One way to find out." He strode over to the alcove and picked up the box. It was light, as if what lay inside had practically no weight. That was promising. A tiny padlock held the box closed, so he handed it to Bones. "You work your magic on the lock. I'll see what's inside the pouch."

While Bones set to picking the lock, Maddock opened the pouch and looked inside. There lay a letter on crumbling yellowed paper. He didn't dare touch it, so he shone his light on it and read it aloud.

My Dear Marquis,

I regret that I am unable to leave to you any portion of the treasure left by the man known to many as Blackbeard. The costs of the War of Independence and the operation of this estate have drained what was once a fortune. I leave you, however, what may be the greatest treasure of all- this relic of Christendom. My reservations on that score are well known to you, and I confess that I do not feel worthy to decide its fate. I leave that task to you.

Your faithful servant,
G Washington

"We've found it!" Sterling said.

"Very good," a voice pierced the darkness. "And now you will give it to me."

It was a measure of Edmonia Jennings Wright's skill that she could sneak up on Maddock and Bones even when they expected her at any second. But this time, Maddock and Bones held the cards.

"Let us go or we'll smash the box," Maddock said. "Two thousand-year-old thorns won't stand the weight of a two hundred fifty pound Cherokee."

"Two-twenty," Bones corrected.

"Smash it and you die." Behind Wright, her men fanned out. Maddock recognized Jamison, who looked as though he was ready to open fire at any second. Wright took a few steps toward them. "Was this really your plan? How did you think it would end? If you somehow managed to leave with the crown, my men would hunt you down. If you tried to trade the crown for your lives, you'd have no leverage once it was in my hands." She let out a laugh that froze Maddock's marrow. "You boys don't know how to play the game. Now, hand it to me and I will consider granting you parole, provided you never interfere with the Sons of the Republic again."

"Screw that," Bones said. "We'll take our chances on the run. Put your weapons down and let us leave or this thing is sawdust." He raised the box, ready to smash it."

"No!" Sterling shouted. In an instant, her Glock was pressed against the back of Bones' head. "Give it to her." Her voice sounded faint.

"Sterling, what the hell are you doing?" Bones said.

"I'm sorry. You have to let her have it."

"So that's how you kept catching up with us," Maddock said to Wright. "It wasn't your extensive resources. Sterling was your mole."

"And that's why we got to the journal before you. Sterling ditched us because she thought it was at the Lincoln Memorial." Bones shook his head. "You are a piece of work, Sandra."

"It's not what you think," Sterling pleaded. "They've got my daughter."

Maddock looked at Bones and then at her. "What are you talking about?"

"The Sons of the Republic, they have my daughter."

"You mean they kidnapped her?"

"They didn't kidnap her. My ex-husband's father is one of the most powerful men in Washington and when we divorced my husband got sole custody. They cooked up some crap about how the danger in my job made me a threat to my little girl. Some judge who was a friend of my father-in-law signed off on it."

"So why did you join the Sons of the Republic if they took your daughter?"

"They didn't give me any choice. Having an insider in the park police was valuable to them. As long as I played along, I could have supervised visits. Otherwise, nothing."

Bones was shaking his head. "I'm not buying this. You've got no criminal record and you have a responsible job. No court in the world would cut off contact with a child's mother."

"It would if enough pressure is brought to bear."

Maddock said, "Judges hate to be controlled. It'd have to be someone the judge really wanted to please. Who the hell is your father-in-law, anyway?"

Then a deep voice sounded from behind Wright's men, and Maddock almost wasn't surprised at yet another intrusion. The man had clearly been listening to their conversation.

"Her father-in-law? That would be me."

TWENTY-ONE

Maddock immediately recognized the man who shouldered through the line of Sons of Republic minions to stand beside Edmonia Jennings Wright. He stood six feet tall, narrow of shoulder and thick around the middle. He wore his graying, curly hair cut short, emphasizing his widow's peak. The instant his face became clear in the light, Maddock knew two things. First, that Sterling had been telling the truth.

Second, they were totally screwed.

The man standing in front of him was Morgan Renko. Chief Justice of the United States Supreme Court.

Bones apparently recognized him, too. "Judge Wapner, I presume?"

Renko scowled. "Sandra, disarm these men and put all the weapons on the ground. Yours too." He waited for Sterling to obey and then turned to Bones. "Give me the crown, or this not only ends badly for the three of you, but for the little girl, too."

"You wouldn't kill your own granddaughter," Bones said.

Ransom's smile turned Maddock's stomach.

"It would be a wrench, that's for certain, but some things are more important than any single life. Not mine, not Edmonia's, not even my granddaughter's. Now, hand me the box."

He held out a hand, smooth and supple, probably never having seen an honest day's work.

"Do it," Maddock said.

Bones handed the box to Renko, who took it carefully. He looked at Maddock. "Do you know how long people have been searching for this?"

Maddock couldn't hold back. "I know how long people have been killing to find artifacts associated with the greatest messenger of peace the world has ever known. You're just the latest in a long line of hypocritical thugs."

"On the contrary, Maddock. The difference is that I've actually found it. And I will use it for good, to restore America to her former greatness. This will inspire millions to return to their Christian roots. To be more ethical. To be less interested in what's in it for them and more interested in their fellows. We'll put the proper people on the bench, in Congress, even in the White House, and the people will thank us for it."

Bones whistled. "Dude, you sound like a twelve step program. Which part of America's former greatness do you want to return to? Is slavery on that list? Or you could slaughter my people again, but there aren't enough of us left for that to even be worth it."

"Enough!"

When Renko yelled, Maddock recognized the temper which had made him legendary on the bench of the Supreme Court. He had been a surprise nominee, a political independent who never failed to speak his mind. The Senate leadership had been girding for a battle with a president who was a member the opposite party, and Renko had sailed through confirmation before they knew what hit them. The half a dozen years since had seen him dominate the court's proceedings like no other justice in history, tearing apart the attorneys unfortunate enough to argue before him, and revealing some decidedly authoritarian positions.

Bones had already picked the lock. Renko's hands trembled as he removed it, loosened the latch, and slowly opened the top. The triumphant look on his face made Maddock want to puke. Until the look transformed into one of immense anger. "What the hell is this?"

"What is it?" Wright asked, turning to peer inside the box.

"Look for yourself." Renko held the box out so everyone could see inside.

The box was lined with mold-specked felt, and in the center, secured by a bit of copper wire, was a rusted metal spike.

"Where is the Crown of Thorns?" Renko took a step toward Maddock. "What have you done with it?"

"Done with it? We followed the clues to Blackbeard's Treasure and that box is what we found."

"But the clues," Renko stammered. "Pierced the flesh of the savior... this isn't..."

Maddock couldn't suppress a laugh. "It's just a relic. Catholic churches all over Europe used them to impress and even control their congregants. At one time there were enough pieces of the alleged true cross and nails that pierced Jesus' palms out there to build an ark. I'm guessing this is one of those alleged nails."

"This could be the real thing," Renko said, a faint trace of hope in his voice.

Maddock shrugged. "Maybe, but probably not. How would you prove it?"

"This can't be," Wright fumed.

"You know, that was the problem with your plan all along. Even if you found the real Crown of Thorns, how would you prove to the masses that it wasn't a fake? At best it would be another Shroud of Turin—some would believe, but most would think it a curiosity or a forgery."

"That thing is legit," Bones said. "So is the Yeti."

"You might have used the treasure to advance your agenda, but Washington spent that. So all you're left with is a useless spike."

Renko flung the box to the ground in disgust. He appeared to think for a moment before settling on something. When his gaze focused on Maddock again, the anger had disappeared. "Unfortunately, I believe you."

Maddock tensed. Renko must have noticed because he chuckled. "Worried about what I'll do next? You can relax Maddock. I'm not going to kill you."

He looked at Sterling. "You failed, Sandra. I don't think it's wise for your daughter to see you again."

Sterling tried to jump toward him, but Jamison fired a shot at her feet, stopping her in her tracks.

"Farewell," Renko said. "Forever."

"Don't bet on it," Bones said. "I don't forgive and I don't forget."

"You misunderstand. *I* am not going to kill you, but you are going to die. You're going to be crushed beneath several tons of earth and stone when Edmonia's men set off the charges they've rigged up above. Nice and clean. Just another of those pesky underground caverns finally giving way. Nothing the good people at Mount Vernon would ever bother to investigate." Renko paused. "You're thinking of your lady friend who will wonder where you've gone." He glanced over his shoulder. "Bring her in."

Maddock's stomach lurched. If Renko had Melissa, Maddock would fight them all with his bare hands if necessary. Whatever it took to get her free. He glanced at the floor where their weapons lay at Wright's feet. The old woman's gaze met his, and a fierce challenge glinted in her eyes.

Try it, she mouthed.

Maddock saw movement behind Wright's men, and a familiar face appeared.

But it wasn't Melissa.

The new arrival was an attractive woman with olive skin, dark hair, and arresting green eyes. She wore dark, form-fitting clothing, body armor, and a badge draped around her neck. She held an automatic pistol. Behind her came a line of men in full combat regalia.

Wright's men turned about but immediately lowered their weapons at the sight of half a dozen automatic rifles trained on them.

"Sorry to break up this party, but you're all under arrest."

"Who are you?" Renko spat.

"Alex Vaccaro. FBI." She glanced at Wright. "Don't expect your men on the grounds to save you. We've taken them all into custody. Some of them are already offering to tell all they know about you."

"Thank God," Renko said. "These people are part of a terrorist organization called the Sons of the Republic. They kidnapped me and brought me here. They've been manipulating me and my daughter-in-law. They've even infiltrated the Navy SEALs." He pointed at Maddock and Bones.

Sterling began to protest but Vaccaro raised a hand to forestall her.

"Justice Renko, one of my men will escort you out. You'll need to tell us all you know about these Sons of the Republic." Renko hurried out, assuring her that he would do all he could to help.

Bones looked from Alex to Maddock, an incredulous smile painting his face. "You called Vaccaro?"

Formerly of Naval Intelligence, Vaccaro had once joined Maddock and Bones on a search for a different treasure. She had since moved on to the FBI, and she and Maddock had kept in touch.

Maddock nodded. "Back in the cave, when you mentioned the Templars, it brought her to mind. Sorry I didn't tell you, but Sterling was sticking so close to us I was lucky I got away long enough to make the call. As soon as Edmonia admitted she had a major government player on her team, I knew we'd never be free unless we could bring these guys down, and for that we needed help." He reached inside his jacket and took out a digital recorder. "And evidence."

"So you got it?" Alex asked as her men took Wright's minions into custody.

"Everything. By the way, how long were you going to wait?"

"I was right around the corner the whole time. I heard everything. Between this tape, our combined testimony, and whatever details Renko spills, we should be able to put him and Ms. Wright here away for a long time."

Wright, who had been standing quietly in the center of the room, sprang into action. Even expecting it, Maddock was surprised at the speed of her attack. She struck him on the wrist, sending the recorder flying. Bones caught it in mid-air and tossed it to Alex before it could be damaged.

Maddock blocked the flurry of kicks and punches Wright threw at him and countered with a punch that she easily dodged.

"Your technique needs work," she scolded. "I..."

A fist flew out of the darkness, clocking her across the temple. Wright's eyes rolled back in her head, her legs turned to rubber, and she collapsed to the floor.

"Thanks, Bones," Maddock said.

"Wasn't me. I don't hit chicks and I don't sucker punch unless it's absolutely necessary."

"I think I broke my hand," Sterling said. She looked at Maddock with pleading eyes. "I hope that, even if you can't forgive me, you'll at least be able to understand why I did what I did."

"I get it," Maddock said.

Sterling nodded and turned to Alex, who was busy handcuffing the unconscious Wright. "Is there any chance you can help me get my daughter back?"

Alex nodded. "We'll get on it immediately." She turned to her men. "Get everyone out of here, and then bring Melissa Moore down here. She's eager to see Maddock. Lord knows why." She winked at Maddock.

As the Sons of the Republic were escorted out of the chamber, Jamison scowled at Maddock. "I'll make you pay for this. You and everyone you care about."

"Have fun in prison," Bones said. "Don't drop the soap."

When the four of them were alone, Vaccaro flashed a sad smile at Maddock. "Once again, you make it to the end of the rainbow, only to find the pot of gold is empty."

Maddock grinned. "Not necessarily."

The others turned triple frowns his way.

"There's something unusual about the letter Washington left for Lafayette. Come take a look." They returned to the alcove and huddled close together so they could see the letter. "See how, here and there, a letter is slanted in the direction opposite the others? Put them together and see what they spell."

Sterling read the letters aloud. *"u-n-d-e-r-t-h-e-g-u-a-r-d. Under the guard?"*

"The guard? There was mention of a guard in Washington's letter to Lafayette. I remember Jamison specifically mentioned it," Bones said. "Does it mean the skeleton?"

"No, he wouldn't want Lafayette to get skewered. I think he means this guard." Maddock shone his light into the alcove on the carving of the soldier standing at attention. Maddock brushed away the dust and mold, revealing a large keyhole.

"If that's the keyhole, where's the key?" Sterling asked.

"I have a hunch," Maddock said. "Somebody grab Edmonia's copy of Bastille key. It's hanging from her belt."

Bones unhooked it and handed it to Maddock. "Looks like a fit to me."

"That it does," Maddock agreed.

"Wait for me." Melissa had arrived and ran into Maddock's arms. After a long embrace, she drew away and gazed up at him. "Don't you think a Mount Vernon staff member should be the one to open it?"

"Absolutely." He handed her the key and they all watched in silent anticipation as she inserted it into hole. It clicked home but nothing happened.

"Try turning it," Bones offered.

"Are you sure? I don't want to break it."

"Go for it," Maddock said.

Slowly, Melissa gave the key a clockwise turn until a series of loud, metallic clanks filled the room. The back wall of the alcove swung forward, revealing a small wooden chest. Melissa grabbed hold of it and pulled, but it scarcely budged. "It's heavy."

"I got this." With more care than he usually took with anything, Bones slid the chest out of the alcove and sat it on the floor. He deftly picked the lock and opened the lid.

"Wow!" Alex breathed.

A rainbow of colors shone on the walls and ceiling as their flashlights danced on gemstones, pearls, and gold coins.

"It's only a fraction of the original treasure," Maddock said, "but at least he kept something for Lafayette."

"There's a pouch there." Sterling picked up a small, leather bag stuffed with gold. On the outside, someone had burned the words, *"For Billy Lee."*

"So he didn't forget Billy after all," Bones said.

"This," Alex said, "is amazing. And I thought busting the Chief Justice was going to be the highlight of my day." She reached out and rested her hands on Maddock's and Bones' shoulders. "Boys, I have to say, you always make things interesting."

End

About the Authors

David Wood is the author of the popular action-adventure series, The Dane Maddock Adventures, as well as several stand-alone works and two series for young adults. Under his David Debord pen name he is the author of the Absent Gods fantasy series. When not writing, he co-hosts the Authorcast podcast. David and his family live in Santa Fe, New Mexico. Visit him online at www.davidwoodweb.com.

Edward G. Talbot is the pen name for two authors. Ed Parrot lives in Massachusetts and has long been fascinated with turning ideas into written words. Jason Derrig lives in Maine and likes to tell stories, especially about conspiracies. The two authors have collaborated to create a brand of thriller that keeps the stakes high while not taking itself too seriously.

In addition to Liberty, their work includes the conspiracy thriller novelsNew World Orders and 2012: The Fifth World. Their most recent books are the terrorism thriller short novels Alive from New York and Alive From America. Click here for a sample of Alive from New York.

Visit him on the web at www.edwardgtalbot.com

www.ingramcontent.com/pod-product-compliance
Lightning Source LLC
Chambersburg PA
CBHW020400130626
46549CB00006B/2368